3

THE DAYSTAR VOYAGES

ESCAPE FROM THE RED COMET

GILBERT MORRIS
AND DAN MEEKS

MOODY PRESS
CHICAGO

ISBN: 0-8024-4107-6

1 3 5 7 9 10 8 6 4 2

Printed in the United States of America

I dedicate this book to my mother,
Lareece Kelly Meeks.

There has never been a day that I've not known my mother's love. She has been a true example of Jesus Christ to me and to everyone else she knows. Most of what I am today is due to her unfailing prayers and sacrifice. She is a person of spiritual wisdom, grounded common sense—and a keen sense of humor! I pray the Lord will bless her mightily.

I love you!
—Danny

Contents

1

Just Give Me the Cash

There's a rat!"

Ringo Smith had been stirring his mug of passion fruit juice with a spoon when, upon looking up, he was shocked to see a purple rat leap over the bulkhead into the *Daystar* mess hall.

Actually it was more the size of a mouse than a rat, but the purple color somehow made it seem larger—and scarier.

Ringo shot a glance at the girl who sat across from him and quickly said, "Don't be afraid, Raina. I'll get rid of him."

Raina St. Clair was fourteen, the same age as Ringo. She had auburn hair with a widow's peak, an oval face, and a faint dimple in her chin—which she claimed to hate. Her green eyes seemed to sparkle. At his words she said, "Yes, do that. Please. I hate rodents."

Jumping up, Ringo snatched an old space magazine from the table and rolled it into a clumsy club. Purposefully, he started across the mess hall, his eyes fixed on the purple rat. Actually, he hoped that the vermin would run away.

Instead, without warning, a purple blur sprang at him.

Startled, Ringo dropped the magazine and scrambled up onto one of the seats built into the bulkhead. "The thing's crazy," he shouted.

Indeed, the rat did seem to be demented. He—or

she—ran around and around the mess hall, uttering a series of high-pitched squeaks.

Raina had drawn her feet up onto her chair, but by now she was giggling. "You'd better use your Neuromag on that beast, Ringo," she told him.

That did a good job of irritating Ringo. He dashed to a locker and snatched out a broom. Soon he was thrashing away at the rat, but the animal managed to evade every blow.

Now Raina was laughing aloud. He saw she was standing on her chair to watch his furious efforts to dispose of the rat.

Ringo finally planted himself firmly in front of the ball of purple fur, stared straight into its pink eyes, and growled, "All right. If you'll just be still, I'll get you this time." He raised the broom, but the rat seemed to know what was coming. It ran straight to Ringo's feet. It made a wild lunge and took hold of his uniform pant leg with its sharp claws.

Ringo yelled, "Get off me! Get off! Get off!" He dropped the broom and fell over backwards in his effort to get away. Flat on his back, he saw the rat crouch. He could see the tiny muscles in the beast's legs. He could see its sharp teeth. Desperately, he made an ineffectual shield of his hands, but he knew that it was hopeless.

And then it happened. The purple rat suddenly began to rise in the air! Its claws dug into the fabric of Ringo's pant leg, but the power that pulled it upward was too great. Slowly but steadily it rose, its four paws waving wildly. It seemed to be swimming in midair.

Ringo scrambled to his feet, gaping at the rat, which was now suspended about four feet from the deck. He thought to glance at Raina, and he saw that she was concentrating on the rat. An intense frown set her features. Her eyes were focused and her fists clenched as she leaned forward, apparently every ounce of her mental powers concentrated on the purple ball of fur.

"Open the disposal port, Ringo," she ordered.

Ringo looked around wildly. Then he leaped to the bulkhead. He unscrewed the port lock and swung the round port open. After that, he stepped back and watched in amazement as the rat slowly moved through the air and exited through the port.

Ringo heard Raina expel her breath. Then he heard a soft plop somewhere outside the ship and the scrambling of tiny feet.

Turning to Raina, Ringo stared. "How did you *do* that?"

Raina always said she didn't like to talk about her strange implant. It was called a kinesthetic enhancer, and its ability frightened her at times—its ability to move objects by the power of her mind. When she was a small child, her parents were missionaries on the planet Zacor. The Zacorians were a brutal, savage, and dangerous race. In those days, when requested, a team of Intergalactic scientists would surgically implant brainwave enhancers that enabled the citizens of the planet to move objects in order to protect themselves. Her parents chose not to have the devices implanted in themselves, but they knew that little Raina needed all the protection they could give her. It had taken many years for her to control the enhancer instead of the enhancer's controlling her! Now she tried never to use it. She didn't even want to talk about it, but the implanted ability was still there.

"Just shut the porthole, Ringo—before he comes back in."

Ringo wagged his head in wonder as he fastened

the port, then came to sit opposite her again. He didn't say anything for a moment. When he did speak, even then he could only say in an awestruck voice, "I wish I could do that."

"I'm not sure you'd like it, Ringo. I *don't*."

Ringo had strong feelings for Raina St. Clair. He enjoyed spending time alone with her like this, just talking.

People told Ringo that he had nice hazel eyes and a straight nose, but he considered himself homely. He did realize that he was a computer expert, even at his young age. Still, as he looked at Raina, he felt inadequate, and he nervously ran a hand over his brown hair.

"And it's not just you. *All* the rest of the Rangers can do something important. All I can do is run a dumb computer."

"But that's important!" Raina protested. "This space cruiser practically runs on computers. You and Heck keep things going." She smiled at him encouragingly.

Ringo thought she looked tired, as if the episode with the rat had drawn physical strength from her. In any case, obviously she did not want to talk about this unusual ability that she had.

"Any word from the top?" a voice sounded.

Raina and Ringo looked up to see Dai Bando enter the mess hall.

Dai, at sixteen, was the oldest of the Space Rangers aboard the cruiser *Daystar*. Certainly he was by far the most striking-looking. He had the blackest hair possible and black eyebrows that arched over his dark eyes. He was just under six feet and weighed one hundred seventy-five pounds, without an ounce of fat. Even as he walked toward them, something of his strength, agility, and quickness came across to Ringo.

10

Dai sat opposite Raina and asked again, "Any word from Commandant Lee?"

"Not yet, as far as we know," she said. She leaned toward him, and something in her smile revealed that she was happy to see Dai Bando.

Ringo could see that.

"I suppose we'll just have to wait," she went on. "What have you been doing this morning, Dai?"

"Oh, working out with Lieutenant Jaleel."

"You're the only one that can stand up against that woman!" Raina said admiringly.

Somehow, Ringo took this as a slight. It was true he could not cope with the weapons officer. Who could —except Dai? Jaleel was almost six feet tall and had features fierce enough to frighten any normal person. He dreaded the sessions in which she taught martial arts. She customarily pounded on him until he was black and blue all over.

Dai ignored Raina's compliment. He just leaned back in his chair and frowned a little. "I wonder what our next mission is going to be. I just hope it won't be to another spooky planet like the last one."

"So do I," she said. "I'd like to take a nice, easy cruise with no problems."

"I don't think we're likely to get that with Commandant Winona Lee in charge." Dai grinned. "I've an idea she lies awake nights thinking of hard stuff for us to do."

Ringo felt closed out of the conversation. In the first place, he always felt inadequate in Dai Bando's presence. Though Dai was not super smart, he had other gifts. He was strong beyond imagination, his reflexes were quick as a light beam, and he had a beautiful singing voice that everyone loved. As Ringo sat listening to them talk, he wished again that he had at least one quality that would hold Raina's attention as Dai was holding it now.

Finally Ringo just got up and went out. He doubted that Raina even noticed when he left the mess hall.

"What do you think of the new equipment, Heck?" Jerusha Ericson asked.

When Heck Jordan didn't answer immediately, she turned to look at him questioningly. He appeared to be pulling apart some complicated apparatus. Jerusha studied him for a moment, thinking, *Heck certainly doesn't look happy. He hardly ever looks happy. He would be a lot happier if he'd just get his values changed around.*

Hector Jordan, always called Heck, was fifteen years old. He had nice-looking red hair and blue eyes, but he was overweight, for he was always eating. Even now as he worked on the device before him, he pulled a candy bar from his pocket, split it in two, and popped one half into his mouth. He chewed with obvious enjoyment.

"To answer your question," he said, "I guess it's all right. But it's got to be better than this. We're liable to meet up with the *Jackray*, and you know what that means."

"What do you know about Sir Richard Iron's ship?" Jerusha asked him.

Heck recited information about Irons's space cruiser as if he were reading an Intergalactic report. "The *Jackray* is three times larger than *Daystar*. It uses Mark IV Star Drive engines. The *Jackray* has sensor arrays, a Neuromag cannon, sophisticated communications equipment, deflectors, turbo cannon, and a space docking port. Rumor has it that Irons has installed an illegal stealth device aboard her, but Intergalactic has not confirmed this."

Still chewing the candy bar vigorously, he winked mischievously at Jerusha, then gave her a slight smile. "Thankfully, *Jackray* is smaller than Commandant Winona Lee's Magnum Deep Space Cruisers. But she's sure not smaller than *us*."

He started feeling his pocket for more of the candy bar. "I know Sir Richard Irons has spent a fortune on it, and I think he did it mostly so he can catch up with the *Daystar* and blast us out of space. That man is some mean cat!"

"I don't doubt that he is," Jerusha said. She came over to watch Heck as he worked. She was fifteen, with ash blonde hair and very dark blue eyes set in a squarish face. People always said there was something not only attractive about Jerusha but something very strong as well. She considered herself competitive, and it showed in her expression. She was, in fact, a very tough young lady. She was also an engineering genius.

"I'll tell you what, Jerusha," Heck said, stuffing the other half of the candy bar into his mouth and talking around it. "The *Daystar* needs to be able to scan the *Jackray* at a much farther distance than we can scan now."

"Can you do anything about that?" Jerusha asked skeptically. She seriously doubted that Heck could make their long-range scanners perform any better. After all, they were already state-of-the-art from the commandant's Intergalactic Fleet. Everybody said they were the best scanners in existence.

Heck looked over the sensor array, picked up the part that he had created, and held it up for Jerusha to see. "Do you know what this little thing is?"

Jerusha studied the small, rectangular circuit board in Heck's hand. "It looks similar to the circuit boards in the scanning unit," she replied.

"Ah, *contraire!*" Heck's eyes sparkled.

Jerusha knew that he sensed her uncertainty.

"This device never existed before last night," he said.

Jerusha also knew that Heck was starting to show off. Still, the only way she was going to learn about this new gadget involved putting up with his monumental ego. "Heck," she said in her helpless-female voice, "you'll have to tell me. What is it?"

Heck Jordan thought no one really appreciated his ability with electronics. Sure, Ringo was a computer genius, and Jerusha was a capable engineer, but she was positive he thought neither of them was as good as he was with electronic components. Heck honestly believed he was the best, and this belief did a lot to fuel his ego.

He held the contraption close to Jerusha's eyes. "Tell me what you see mounted in the middle of the board." He smiled with admiration for himself.

Jerusha squinted as she focused her eyes on the mounting at the board's center. "It looks like glass to me. What is it?" But even as the words came out of her mouth, she knew the answer. "Heck— that's *tridium!*"

Heck laughed out loud. "You guessed it!"

"Where'd you get it? I thought all the tridium on board was in the captain's safe."

"It is. All but this piece."

The engineering side of Jerusha took over, and her voice turned from helpless female to excited.

Clearly, all this was not lost on Heck. He knew admiration when he saw it, and he appeared to be relishing every second of it. "I won't tell you *how* I got it— just that I did! You're looking at one of the most valuable circuit boards in existence because of the tridium." Heck began to sound like a professor. "It's too complicated to explain how it works right now—just let me tell you that it increases our long-range scanners by one-third."

"One-third!" Jerusha exclaimed. "If that's true, that makes *Daystar*'s long-range scanner more powerful than any other, *including* Richard Irons's *Jackray*. That's wonderful, Heck!"

Heck Jordan's chest swelled with pride. "I still have a couple of bugs to work out, but it should be operational later today." Then he scratched his chin, thought for a moment, and scowled. "And, Jerusha, my guess is that Irons knows about tridium's value electronically. I have only a tiny speck of it here. Imagine what Irons could do if he got a full shipment of the mineral!"

Jerusha listened to Heck talk on and on about Sir Richard Irons. She knew Irons was a space pirate—a wealthy space pirate, though, which made things different. His controlling aim was to become the head of the Intergalactic Council, and he would stop at nothing to accomplish that goal.

Jerusha thought, suddenly, how life had changed for all the Rangers. Commandant Lee had come up with the funds to install the latest equipment on the *Daystar*, and—now that the work was done—the young ensigns known as the *Daystar* Space Rangers expected her to send them on a mission.

They were all—except for Dai—rejects from the Intergalactic Space Academy. For one reason or another they had been expelled, some because they were Christians, others because they would not fit into the rigid rules of the Academy.

She said abruptly, "Heck, do you like being a Space Ranger?"

"I'd like it if I were captain." He grinned. "Someday

I'll put Edge out of a job"—Mark Edge, captain of the *Daystar*. Heck glanced over his shoulder quickly to be sure that no one had overheard him. "He's a hard man. I could do a better job as captain."

Jerusha thought of Edge, and something in her face must have changed.

"You still have a crush on him, don't you?" Heck said slyly.

"Don't be foolish! He's twenty-five years old. Besides, he hasn't had time for *any* of us since Dr. Cole came on board."

"Can't blame him for that. She's some dish." He grinned again. "Say, speaking of great love affairs, I've about decided to give Raina a break. She needs to have the best, and that's me."

Jerusha could not help but smile. Heck Jordan had an ego practically as large as the *Daystar*. He loved fancy clothes and considered himself a ladies' man. No matter how many rebuffs he got, it never seemed to disturb him.

"What do you think, Jerusha? When I get enough cash, she'll fall right in my hands, don't you think so?"

"No, I don't think so, Heck."

"What are you talking about? Women always go for the guys with the money."

"There are more things than money in this world! Girls know that."

"Just give me the cash." Heck pulled a part out of the machine he was working on and grunted with satisfaction. "Here it is. This is what I've been looking for." Then he glanced again at Jerusha and bobbed his head. "I know what you're going to say. You're gonna preach me a sermon."

Jerusha smiled again. She was truly fond of Heck, but she knew that he was headed the wrong way. "If you don't have the right relationship with God through Christ, all the money in the world won't help you, Heck," she said seriously.

He looked uncomfortable. He'd always said he didn't like to be preached at, and he was infinitely greedy for what he called the "finer things in life."

Unexpectedly, he reached over, grabbed Jerusha's hair, and pulled her face close to his. "Hey, sweetheart. You're going to love me when I make my million. All I have to do is get the captain to haul us back to Makon and get some of that tridium."

Jerusha would never forget the time Edge had taken the *Daystar* to Makon, the one planet that produced a rare mineral harder than diamonds. Undoubtedly, it would make rich anyone who could market it.

Heck released Jerusha's hair when she pulled away, and he went on voicing his hopes. "I sure would like to have about a zillion dollars. Then I'd show you what living is!"

"No, Heck, you wouldn't!" Jerusha said, thinking how sad it was that he was so caught up with the desire for money.

But she couldn't help thinking, *Still, money sure comes in handy from time to time.*

2

What About Angels?

Ensign Ericson, report to the bridge at once!"
Captain Edge's voice blared over the loudspeaker system, and Jerusha Ericson jumped. "I've got to go, Heck."

"All right, but I'll see you later." He winked at the blonde ensign and said, "Me and you, we're gonna have to get together. You hear me?"

Heck laughed as Jerusha stuck her nose in the air and left engineering at once.

Turning to the new circuit board that had just been added to the long-range scanner equipment, Heck lifted the lid on a small wooden box. He reached in and almost reverently removed a shiny piece of new equipment that would fit on the module. It was no larger than a penny.

Now I'll just add to the circuit board this one piece that Jerusha knows nothing about, Heck thought, humming to himself. He never liked to give away all his secrets. *This little gadget is the only thing that will allow the tridium circuit board to link with the long-range scanner.*

Once the device was in place, Heck said, "Now, sweetheart, you're going to treat me right, aren't you? Sure, you are." He had the habit of talking to his equipment, sometimes under his breath, sometimes shouting at the top of his lungs. Now he was pleased at the sound of his quiet question as the computer whistled and chirped out a musical melody.

"That's right!" Heck exclaimed. "You know I'm talkin' to you, don't you? You and me, we're gonna make history together."

Again the computer made the whistling, chirping sound that was almost like a song.

Heck beamed. He tinkered with the device a bit more. "You know," he whispered confidentially, "I'm the one Raina's gonna fall for. You know that, don't you?"

Whistle!

Chirp!

"Sure. I'm gonna make the cash, and when I get those new threads I got my eye on, she's gonna love me! Right?"

Whistle!

Chirp!

He grinned with satisfaction as the device seemed to be answering him.

"After all," he went on, making minor adjustments and then squinting at the machinery, "Dai Bando, what's he? He's all muscle. Nothing between the ears, you know."

Whistle!

Chirp!

"And that Ringo. Why, he's a *nothing!* Aw, he can run a computer, but so what? He doesn't have what I've got."

The computer gave off a harsh croak.

Heck jerked his hand back. "Hey, what's the matter with you? I'm telling you I'm a great guy!"

The computer uttered a series of abusive squawks that hurt Heck's ears. He reached out and slapped the computer housing. "Stop that!" he said. "You're supposed to talk sweet to me! I have to put up with that kind of guff all day from the rest of the Rangers!"

Heck was, in fact, a strange young man, perhaps

the most unusual of all the Rangers. He was totally self-ish, and his favorite saying was "You got to look out for number one."

He picked up his tools and began working again on the long-range scanner. He was humming under his breath, for he really was happiest when he was working on some sort of invention or new piece of machinery that was a challenge to his talents.

Then he began whistling softly as he made further minute adjustments to the computer. He delighted in the little chirps and whistles that it uttered from time to time. He was in his element.

But when he gazed up again at the scanner display, Heck Jordan sat absolutely still for a moment. Next, he uttered what sounded like a half cough and a half sneeze. And then Heck let out a full-fledged yelp. *"What in the world!"*

What he saw was an enormous red comet.

Initial data from the new long-range scanners confirmed that this was indeed a comet. But instead of its being white with a white tail streaming from it, this comet and its tail were red. Being the size of Saturn, the comet appeared huge, even though it was still many light-years away.

Heck did a few computations on the navigational computer.

"This big baby is heading straight for us!" he whispered to himself.

As soon as he had assured himself that what he was seeing was real, he touched the switch on the communications panel and said sharply, "Engineering to bridge!"

"Edge speaking."

"I found something that I've never seen before, Captain."

"What is it—a bug-eyed monster from some distant planet?"

"No, I'm serious, Captain. I'm looking at the hugest comet you ever saw. It's red as a tomato and bigger than you can believe—and it's headed right for us!"

Capt. Mark Edge listened to Heck babble on about what he was seeing. The young captain was a rather skeptical man, as most captains had to be. He looked the role, too. He had blond hair and light blue-gray eyes that could bore through someone like a laser. He looked, in fact, like the Viking he had practically been at one time, before assuming command of the *Daystar*.

Skeptical or not, Edge turned to his first officer, Zeno Thrax. "First, I think you'd better go down to engineering and see what Ensign Jordan is talking about."

"Aye, sir."

Zeno Thrax was probably the most exceptional-looking member of the *Daystar* crew. He was a perfect albino, having white hair and colorless eyes, and was rather chilling to look at. He came from the planet Mentor Seven, where the entire population lived underground. Zeno was also a mystery man. He had never explained to *Daystar*'s crew why he left his home planet. He had been cut off from his people. Nevertheless, he was a fine first officer. He left the bridge at once, passing Jerusha Ericson with a nod of his head.

As Jerusha entered the bridge, Captain Edge greeted her with a question. "Have you been with Heck, Ensign Ericson?"

"I just left him."

"Did you see anything on that new equipment of his?"

"No, he was still working on it when I left."

Edge studied the ensign for a few more seconds, and then his lips turned upward in a wry smile. "Well, I think he's gone out of his mind. He's talking about some enormous red comet that seems to be heading for us. Whoever heard of a *red* comet? I think he just wants some attention down there."

"That could be, sir. Heck is a very lonely young man. I feel sorry for him."

"Sorry for him? I feel like drowning him. Along with that dog of yours." The captain looked around behind Jerusha suspiciously. "She's not with you, is she?"

"No. Contessa's taking a nap in my quarters."

Contessa was her German shepherd, a super breed, black as night and bred for intelligence. She loved Jerusha and no one else—except for Captain Edge. For some reason she was enamored of the captain, and Edge hated all dogs.

"You ought to show a little more kindness to Contessa," Jerusha ventured. "She loves you so much."

"Just keep her away from me," Edge said testily. "She's so big she knocks me down with all of her love and affection!" But then he grinned, and his rugged good looks were obvious. "I'm just kidding. I can put up with the beast, I suppose. You blackmailed me to get her on this ship, anyhow."

"I couldn't leave her on Earth, Captain." Jerusha enjoyed being with Captain Edge. Although she had had her difficulties with him at first, she had learned to trust and respect him as a captain. She had never seen anyone more capable of commanding a star cruiser.

But more than respect was involved, Jerusha

knew. Mei-Lani Lao, perhaps her closest friend on board the *Daystar*, had once told her, "You've got the world's biggest crush on Captain Edge, and it's going to get you in trouble." Unfortunately, others had noticed, too—even Heck, who teased her about it constantly.

"How are you doing, Jerusha?" Edge asked in friendly fashion. "I don't see much of you anymore."

She thought of saying, *You haven't seen me—or anyone else, for that matter—since Temple Cole came on board.* Dr. Temple Cole—the surgeon who had been assigned by Commandant Lee to the *Daystar* as medical officer. And despite herself, Jerusha again felt a twinge of jealousy. Temple Cole was a beautiful woman by anyone's standards. She was exactly the same age as Mark Edge.

"I'm doing very well, sir," she told him.

"Have you spent any time with Dr. Cole?"

The unexpected question caught Jerusha off guard. "Why, no . . . not really." As a matter of fact, she disliked Temple Cole and didn't want to spend time with her. But she could never quite figure out if it was because she was jealous or if the woman just seemed cold and unfeeling. "She gave me a vitamin shot a couple of days ago. That's all."

Edge fiddled with some dials on the board. "I hate shots. I avoid them whenever possible."

"I suppose everyone does. No one likes them. But they're a lot better now than they used to be. In the old days they would stick a needle in you. Now, with the use of hyper-epidermic intromitters, it's not so bad."

"I don't care what way they give them! Either the old needle way or the new micro sprays." Edge snorted. "I just don't like anybody tampering with my body!" Then he focused on the console before him, as though preoccupied with the new devices that had been installed at the refitting of the ship. But at last he turned back to her and said, surprisingly, "You're growing up, Ensign Ericson."

"Thanks a lot, sir. I'm glad you noticed."

Edge smiled at her sarcasm. "You never did like for me to tease you. It's just that all you Rangers are so young. I feel like an old man with a beard."

"You're not that much older than I am."

"They didn't teach you much about arithmetic at the Academy, did they? You're—what? Fifteen?"

"Almost sixteen!" Jerusha said indignantly, her dark blue eyes daring him to laugh at her.

"That's right. Almost sixteen, and here I am twenty-five. Well, you'll get old, too, one of these days."

Jerusha couldn't hold back a broad smile. "Don't trip over your beard, Captain."

Edge laughed. "All right. I'll do my best not to. Jerusha—" his tone abruptly changed "—I want you to do me a favor."

"Yes, of course," she said eagerly. "I'd be glad to. What is it?"

"It seems to me that Dr. Cole has been isolating herself on this voyage. I'm getting worried about her. I think she's got some kind of a problem."

"I think we all have problems!" Jerusha retorted rather sharply.

Edge was a gifted space cruiser captain, but he was not noticeably adept at picking up signals from young women. When he immediately went on to ask, "Jerusha, has Temple ever said anything to you about me?" she knew that he had not caught the frostiness of her tone.

"No, she hasn't. Not particularly. But I agree—she has seemed preoccupied lately." Jerusha hated the conversation and wanted to leave the bridge. "Well, I'll be about my duties," she said.

"Wait a minute, Jerusha." Edge took her arm and held it for a few seconds. "Here's the favor. Try to talk to Dr. Cole, will you? See if you can find out what's troubling her. Will you do that for me? I'd appreciate it."

She said—though reluctantly—"I'm not much of a psychiatrist or a psychologist, Captain, but I'll talk to her." Jerusha would have agreed to almost anything that Captain Edge asked.

"Thanks, Jerusha. Let me know when you find out something." He turned back and ran his hand over the controls of the console, part of his mind already far out in space.

But Jerusha knew that the other part of Mark Edge's mind was on Temple Cole, and as she turned away from him, she thought, *Why did I ever agree to talk to that woman? I won't do it!*

She knew, however, that she would, and she left the bridge angry and upset.

"No, there's no such thing as an angel!"

Ivan Petroski, the *Daystar*'s chief engineer, was thirty years old. He was, however, only about four and one-half feet tall. He came from the planet Bellinka Two, where he was actually considered to be a rather large man among his people. He had dark brown eyes and very thick curly brown hair. At the moment his sharp-featured face was turned to Dai Bando and Ringo, and he was insisting in a loud voice, "I don't believe in angels!"

"But I'm telling you I saw one," Ringo said. "On the planet Merlina. I'll never forget it. He was dressed in a white robe with a hood, but at times the robe seemed to change into colors that flashed and glowed as he moved. His skin was dark tan and golden. When he looked at me, I can tell you I was terrified, but at the same time I felt such inner calm and peace. The words he spoke to me were not so much spoken out loud as they were . . . I don't know how to describe this, but his words were like . . . like love, somehow—living love that you feel you can touch with your hand."

Ivan threw up his hands and wagged his head back and forth. "Ringo, you must have been drugged. You saw an illusion, not an angel."

Somehow it was important to Ringo that the little man believe him. "I don't know why I was the one picked to see him. I only know that I did. And by the way, he was wearing something else interesting."

"What's that?" Ivan snorted. "Wings?"

"No, I didn't see any wings. He wore a golden cord that hung from his shoulder—"

"So what? A golden cord. A golden cord. This illusion is getting better all the time!"

"It's just that at the end of the cord, located near his waist, was a golden trumpet, Ivan. That trumpet had to mean something. I haven't pieced it all together yet, though." In desperation, Ringo turned to Dai Bando for help.

Dai smiled back at him. He'd been listening as the two argued back and forth.

But before Dai could say a thing, there was a step, and they all turned to see Studs Cagney coming. As always, Dai gave the crew chief a big grin, for Cagney had become a particular friend of his.

Ringo well remembered that it had not always been so. When Dai joined the *Daystar* crew, the crew chief had attempted to rough him up. Short and muscular, rough and brutal, Cagney had come up the hard way. He'd had no interest in God or in people who were interested in God.

But now Studs wiped his hands on an oily rag, and he too listened awhile to the chief engineer loudly proclaiming the nonexistence of angels.

"Why is it so hard for you to believe in angels, Chief?" Studs asked.

"Because I'm a man of science!" Petroski said shortly.

"Why, I don't think it's too hard for a man of science to believe in angels."

"Did *you* ever see one?" Petroski snorted.

"Well, no, but Dai here says that there is such a thing, and Ringo claims he's seen one."

It was a never-ending argument. Dai Bando was a fervent Christian. Ringo was a new believer. But Ivan Petroski was a disbeliever in most spiritual things.

Petroski waved his arms and said in a huff, "If I can't see it or measure it—it doesn't exist! My people are practical people!" He stared into their faces. "I would suggest that the three of you think seriously about this. You can't run a starship on dreams and fantasies!" He stormed away, his back straight.

"Why does the man get hot about believing in angels?" Cagney wondered aloud. He scratched his head, mussed his thinning black hair, and looked puzzled. "I don't see why he has to get so mad about it."

Dai Bando turned to face his friend. "I think, Studs, that he's afraid to believe. If he ever believed in angels—and God—he'd have to give up a lot of his pet ideas."

"Seems to me that's a dumb reason for not believing in God," Studs muttered.

Ringo nodded fervently. "I guess any reason for not believing in God is dumb."

"Well, if we ever get under way, we might find something out there in space that'll change his mind," Studs said. "Maybe Ringo will see some more angels."

Dai grinned. "I don't think there's an angel perched on every star. But I'm praying for Ivan that he'll find the Lord someday—and you too, Studs."

Cagney shifted uncomfortably. "Maybe someday," he said. "Maybe someday." Then he turned and walked off, no doubt thinking about angels.

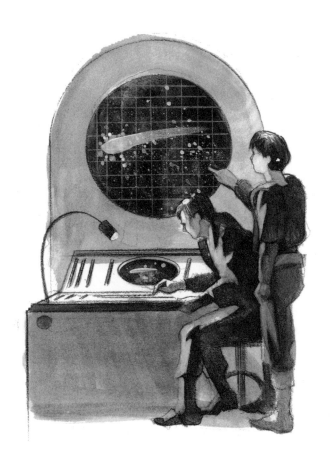

3

Rogue Comet

Zeno Thrax's people did not travel about the galaxy as did other peoples in the Intergalactic system. They preferred to stay on their home planet, Mentor Seven. Of all the planets under the authority of the Intergalactic Council, the Mentorians were, perhaps, the most withdrawn. They did not welcome strangers. Their planet was highly inhospitable. If one liked living underground, never seeing the light of day, he would perhaps like Mentor Seven. But Zeno Thrax was an exile even from his unattractive planet. The first officer was a lonely man.

As Thrax stepped inside the engineering sector and walked over to where Heck Jordan was at work, he was surprised by a sudden thought. *I think Heck and I are the two loneliest people on the Daystar. Neither one of us seems to be able to reach out and be friendly with people the way Raina St. Clair, say, or Dai Bando can.*

And then Zeno had a rash impulse. He thought he would like to strengthen the bond between himself and Heck, although that would be truly difficult for him to do. By nature he was cold and analytical, and what emotions lay in him were buried so deeply that he found it very hard to express his feelings at all.

He tried valiantly, however. He stepped up beside Jordan and tried smiling. "How's it going with the electronics, Heck? Anything new?"

"Oh, hello, Zeno!" Heck barely turned his head

from the long-range scanner. He seemed totally fascinated by what was happening on the screen. In any case, he missed the overture of friendship, such as it was, that Zeno made.

Zeno was aware that Heck Jordan was hungry for recognition. He also knew that the boy was completely self-centered. Zeno himself would not have known self-esteem if he had met it coming across the deck toward him.

Still, he determined to do his best to show Heck friendliness.

Perhaps, Zeno thought, part of the problem was his albino eyes. It was through the eyes that most people express themselves, he had heard. Someone had said a person's eyes were the "mirror of the soul." But his own colorless eyes reflected nothing. They were more like two opaque pieces of ice than anything else.

He tried a compliment. "Well, Ensign, I must commend you for this new scanning device."

"It is a whopper, isn't it, Zeno?"

"It certainly extends our long-range scanning ability by several light-years. We'll badly need it in case we ever encounter Sir Richard Irons—or someone worse."

"I don't think there can be anyone worse than Irons!" Heck exclaimed. Then he leaned toward the screen and narrowed his eyes. "Look here at this red comet, Zeno. Did you ever see anything like it? Look at the area just around the nucleus. Scanners indicate that this comet has a corona. I can just make out the flaring patterns. See? It's very similar to a star's solar flares! But how can a comet have flares?"

Just then, a burst of light that was stronger and longer than the rest erupted from the red comet's surface. The flare reached past the corona boundary, then curved back into the comet.

"Comets are made out of ice!" Heck said in exasperation. "I have no idea what this red comet is made from."

Zeno studied the screen for a time. Then he too shook his head. "No, I never heard of a red comet. I didn't know they existed."

"Well, I can tell you one thing it's going to do."

"What's that, Ensign?"

"It's gonna make big problems for us. That's what."

"What sort of problems?" Zeno well knew what problems, but he wanted to hear how Heck saw the situation.

"Look at this screen." Heck pointed to the outside edge of the scanning field. "See that? That's static."

"I see it is. And it's pretty bad too."

"Bad? Listen, First Officer," Heck said seriously, "that static could wipe out all the computers on board this ship if it gets stronger."

Zeno stated the obvious. "And without the computers we could hardly manage. The whole ship is driven by them."

"Tell me about it! I think what we'd better do is turn around and head out of here."

Bronwen Llewellen, navigator of the *Daystar*, was knitting a sweater. It occurred to her, as the needles clicked and flashed under the fluorescent light over her head, that she was probably the only one aboard the *Daystar* who knew how to knit. It was an ancient art, mostly forgotten now, since space-age machines did all of the necessary weaving.

"I still like something that I make with my own hands," Bronwen murmured to herself.

She reached over and turned on an Audio-ROM of Welsh music. The music device could record anything, and the playback featured full surround-sound quality. She began listening to a folk song sung by her nephew, Dai Bando. As Dai's sweet, clear voice came over the speaker, she lowered her head, and her fingers ceased to move. Like most Welsh songs, it told a sad and poignant story, and Bronwen felt the tears rise to her eyes. She had been away from her native land for many years now, but the voice of the boy and words of the old song brought it all back again.

The door panel chirped, signaling that someone in the corridor outside wanted to visit. Bronwen quickly reached into her pocket, pulled out her handmade handkerchief, and wiped away the tears. "Come in," she said, and the door opened.

"Why, good morning, Zeno." She had formed a firm relationship with the first officer, and the two of them had spent many evenings together. They had decided that they both were rather solitary people. Now she took one look at the face of her friend and knew something was wrong. "Zeno, what is it?"

"We're having some sort of problem, Bronwen. Would you come with me to navigation and have a look?"

Rising, Bronwen put her knitting away and switched off the music.

Thrax smiled. "Do you ever finish one of those things?"

"Oh, yes. This one is for Dai. And I'll be glad to start one for you as soon as I finish. If that's not too ambitious a project at my age."

Zeno Thrax grinned at her. "You're still young at heart, Navigator," he said. "And you have many abilities." He'd once told her that he was particularly fascinated by one of those abilities. She seemed to have what the Welsh called "second sight." Zeno claimed he did not fully understand that because it was not scientific—but he'd acknowledged that sometimes Bronwen did appear to know things that could not be known.

He followed her as she left her cabin, and the door closed silently behind them like the diaphragm of a camera. Then, side by side, they walked without speaking down the corridor and toward the navigation deck.

There, Bronwen sat behind her console, and her fingers flew over the switches.

Watching her, Zeno said, "See that red comet out there, Navigator? Something's very wrong about that."

"Captain Edge told me Heck had pinpointed an unusual comet, so I've been thinking about it," Bronwen said, as she pushed more buttons and flicked more switches. She stared at the large round screen in front of her. "In all my travels, I must say I've never heard of such a thing as a red comet."

"And certainly you've traveled more than most. If *you* haven't heard of it, I doubt if anyone else has."

Bronwen began changing channels on the navigation console. The outermost fringes of the different megahertz ranges were dissipating. Ever so slightly she fine-tuned one of the control bands. The dissipation increased. And then she started to hear static in the background, static of a kind she had never heard before. It sounded like . . . like thousands of crickets. And it was getting louder.

The navigator felt her forehead form worry lines. "We've got big problems, Zeno."

"What is it?"

"There's radiation of some sort out there. It's throwing all of my equipment out of joint."

Zeno leaned over her shoulder and watched lines fragment and scatter on the huge circular screen. "Do you think it could be caused by Heck's red comet?"

"I'm not sure. The comet is still thousands of light-years away, but if it *is* what's causing the problem, the closer it gets to us, the worse the navigational array is going to get." Puzzled and frowning, Bronwen looked up at the first officer. Then she stiffened, and her eyes widened as a flash of insight came to her.

Zeno Thrax's face took on a concerned look. "What is it, Bronwen?" he asked her. "Are you all right?"

"Yes—yes, I'm all right, but I have the impression that something wicked this way comes!"

Capt. Mark Edge was not conceited—no more than most men. However, as he stood in front of the mirror brushing his hair, something caught his attention. His eyes narrowed, and he leaned forward and stared at his hairline. Reaching out a tentative finger, he traced it and muttered, "Don't tell me I'm losing my hair!"

The face that stared back at him from the mirror was wedge-shaped and built for hard usage. Several small scars adorned his features, reminders of a time when he was quicker to use his fists than now. Though he had grown up with a fiery temper, he had learned to keep it under fairly firm control. Those times when his anger did get out of hand rather frightened him.

Now, staring at his blond hair, he scowled but eventually muttered a relieved "Oh, I guess not. A bald-headed captain of a starship? Whoever heard of such a thing?"

The captain pulled on the tunic of his uniform. It was standard issue. The tunic was slate gray with silver trim on the collar and above the cuffs. The captain insignia was located on the right sleeve. The Intergalactic insignia was sewn to the top of the left sleeve. Navy pants with a silver stripe down the sides and black half boots with rubber soles completed the outfit.

Mark turned away from the mirror, crossed to the door, and with his voice activated the opener. He took one step out, only to be struck hard on the chest by an enormous black dog.

"Jerusha!" Edge yelled automatically. He lost his balance and fell backwards into the cabin. The dog immediately sat on his stomach and placed her front paws on his shoulders. She was an immense animal, weighing almost as much as Edge himself. She began to lick his face, now and then yelping happily.

"*Jerusha!* Get this beast off me! Where *are* you?"

"Contessa!"

Jerusha hurried down the corridor and into Captain Edge's cabin. She took one look and tried to conceal her amusement, but she was unsuccessful. Involuntarily, the corners of her mouth curled upward. Nevertheless, seizing the dog by her collar, she commanded firmly, "Contessa, get off the captain!"

Contessa was trained to obey instantly, and she backed off at once. Her tail continued to wag wildly and enthusiastically. Looking down into Edge's face, she growled happily deep in her throat.

Captain Edge tried hard not to lose his dignity as he got up from where he had sprawled on the floor. He brushed at the front of his tunic. "That monster slobbered all over me! Again!"

"I'm sorry, Captain," Jerusha said contritely. "I truly am."

"Well, you should be sorry! Look at this mess!"

"She doesn't take up with anybody else. Except for me, of course." This time Jerusha could not contain her smile. On top of that, she couldn't hold back a giggle. "I've always been told you could trust a man that dogs took to."

"Well, that's arrogant nonsense! I knew a murderer once, and every dog he ever saw loved him."

"Is that right?"

"No, it's not right, but that's the way it was!" Edge glared down at his chest and swiped his forearm across it. "Now I have to go to work with dog slobber all over my uniform! And what are you coming to my cabin for, anyway?"

"You're wanted in the conference room, sir. I was passing by, and they thought it would be easier for me to tell you than to call you on your intercom."

"What is it?"

"Something about that red comet, I believe, sir. Everybody's talking about it."

"Well, talking about it's not going to fix anything!" Edge growled. He still eyed Contessa warily. "And keep that beast away from me! Do you hear? Keep her away, or I'll chunk her out into space!"

"Yes, sir, I will."

Jerusha wasn't worried. She knew that Captain Edge's bark was much worse than his bite, although she'd once said, "It'd be better to get bitten once in a while than to be barked at *all* the time." Besides, she strongly suspected that the captain really had an affection for Contessa but was too stubborn to admit it.

"Well, come with me," he growled. "You may as well hear firsthand what this is all about."

"Yes, Captain."

With a whisper and a gesture of her hand, Jerusha warned Contessa to behave. Then she almost had to trot to keep up with Mark Edge's long strides. She waited for him to ask if she had spoken with Temple Cole yet, but he seemed to have his mind on the problems with the ship.

And that's the way it should be, she thought. *He*

needs to get his mind on his business, not on that woman.

Captain Edge found Zeno Thrax, Ivan Petroski, and Bronwen Llewellen waiting for him in the small conference room. They were seated about an eight-foot round table that the grunts had painted forest green. A command console stood next to the table. All of *Daystar's* systems could be monitored from this console. One light fixture, shaped like a crystal, hung from the ceiling and focused beams of soft light on the table area in front of each place.

The captain and Jerusha each pulled up a chair.

"So what's the word on this red comet, First?"

"Sir," Thrax said, "the comet that Ensign Jordan sighted has begun to create great difficulty with our navigational system."

"Are we still operational, Bronwen?" Edge demanded of his navigator.

"We are, sir. But the closer it gets to us, the more interference we can expect to have with my equipment."

"I think this must be a rogue comet," Ivan Petroski put in. "There's nothing anywhere in the books about a comet like this." He squinted suspiciously at Bronwen Llewellen as if she had created the problem. "Are you certain about this comet, Navigator?"

"Ensign Jordan located it, and it's definitely there. I agree that it must be a rogue comet."

"What are you actually saying, Bronwen?" Edge asked.

"Heck ran a computer inquiry, but that revealed nothing except an old myth about a red comet and the planet Siphius." Bronwen repeated the information that Heck had given her. "The story has to do with a great red comet sent by the gods to punish the people of Siphius. They believed their gods were angry at them because, as they developed more technology, the less time they spent with the gods. The red comet flew very close to the planet, so close that it killed all of the inhabitants." Bronwen cleared her throat. "But further computer analysis fails to pinpoint Siphius's location."

"Well, I'd say that if the comet is a rogue," Zeno Thrax offered, "that's still better than having Sir Richard Irons closing in on us."

"I'm not even sure about that one, Zeno," Captain Edge said thoughtfully. "We can handle Irons, but there's not much any of us can do about a comet. And it's really *red*, Bronwen?"

"Yes, sir. It certainly is." Bronwen Llewellen seemed to ponder the tabletop. "But that's just one of the odd things about it. The other is the way that it is disrupting our equipment."

"What would you recommend, Bronwen?" Edge asked softly.

"I recommend that we land somewhere until the comet's out of the area, sir."

"I think that's wise," Zeno Thrax agreed quickly. "We don't know exactly how much damage that comet will do when it gets closer, and if our computers are powered down, they shouldn't be at risk."

Edge scarcely hesitated. "Very well. Have you chosen a planet for us to land on, Navigator?"

"Yes. It's right here." Bronwen placed her finger on the screen. "This one. The planet Ciephus, which orbits the center star in the Orion belt." The navigator traced a path around the Great Orion Nebula. "As you see, we can steer around Rigel, through the left wing of the nebula, and head directly toward Ciephus. On the way, we might even get lucky and get a good view of the star Orionis. It's hidden in the nebula most of the time."

Edge studied the screen. The Great Orion Nebula was green in color. It reminded him of a dove in flight, its wings spread in glorious array. Then his eyes moved up the screen and settled on the star Alnilan. "What do we know about Ciephus?"

Bronwyn examined her database. "It is thought to be the only planet orbiting this star that can support human life. The planet once had colonists. They lived in a few cities, but most were deserted millenniums ago. We don't really know what is there today, if anything. Ciephus hasn't been visited for almost fifty years."

"Very well. Execute at once." Turning to Jerusha, Captain Edge said, "I want the ship put on alert at once, Ensign Ericson."

"Yes, sir!"

"And talk to Ensign Lao. See if she knows anything about this red comet. She knows everything else, I think." His voice was wry. He well knew that though little Mei-Lani Lao, aged thirteen, was the youngest of the Rangers, her head held an enormous amount of information.

"Yes, sir," Jerusha repeated, getting up. "I'll check with Ensign Lao at once." She paused briefly to comment, "I hope there are no awful beasts on Ciephus like the kind we ran into on our last mission!" She shuddered as she walked off.

Edge too had bad memories of the monstrous, serpentlike creatures on Makon—creatures with tremendous fangs and two grasping arms for seizing their victims. He turned his attention back to the screen. "I think there just could be something worse than a scaly serpent out there," he said.

"I feel that, too, Captain," Bronwen said. Her eyes were clouded, and her face was tense. She was staring at the navigational screen but seemed to be hearing something that was inaudible to the men who stood behind her.

4

A Bout with
Lieutenant Jaleel

D r. Temple Cole sat before the mirror in her cabin. Automatically the recessed lights came on so that she was bathed in their warm, iridescent glow. She began slowly brushing her strawberry blonde hair. It was cut short and was curly, and the doctor was thankful that it was easy to take care of.

Then, satisfied with the hair, she slipped into her sky blue uniform. Simplicity described the uniform—it was just a lightweight syntho-cotton knit shirt and pants. Like their predecessors for hundreds of years before them, the medical personnel aboard star cruisers dressed for comfort and ease of movement.

She pulled on her half boots, stood and took a deep breath, then went out of the dressing room area into the cabin itself. Looking around her living space, she once again thought, *Well, it will have to do. It's nothing like my last quarters, though—I lived in a palace compared to this!*

A small end table sat between two forest green couches along the wall that faced her bed. Being an avid reader, Dr. Cole loved stretching out on one of the couches with a book. Her computer sat on a larger, circular table in the center of the room.

Sitting next to the computer console, a pot of Nectron Forever flowers gave off their sweet honeysuckle aroma. Her previous captain had given her the rare plant on their first date, and she couldn't bear to part with it. The flowers were shaped like day lilies and were emerald green with yellow fringes. They were in perpetual bloom. What made them so rare involved the eight-month cycle of the planet Nectron. Once every eight months, the Nectron Forever flower turned dark red, and for two weeks its scent changed to that of roses. The change in color and fragrance exhilarated the senses.

Temple Cole sat down and picked up a book. It was a very old book, and she turned the pages carefully, almost reverently. It was a book of poems. Having selected a poem written by John Bunyan, she began to read it aloud:

"He that is down, needs fear no Fall;
He that is low, no pride:
He that is humble, ever shall
Have God to be his guide.
I am content with what I have,
Little be it or much:
And, Lord, Contentment still I crave,
Because thou savest such.
Fulness to such, a Burden is,
That go on Pilgrimage:
Here little, and hereafter Bliss,
Is best from Age to Age."

"I wonder why I like old things better than new things?" she murmured. A smile turned up the corners of her lips. "I'd really rather be far back in time, crossing the American plains in a prairie schooner, than going across the skies in a star cruiser." But then she laughed aloud. "No, actually I wouldn't. I'd die of boredom after a day."

Temple gently set aside the book and wandered over to the port, where she stood and stared out at the canopy of space. Beyond the cruiser's window a myriad stars glittered against the velvety blackness. As always, the view thrilled her, while the ship chopped through infinite space without the least sensation of movement.

The door chime sounded, and she turned from the port.

"Enter."

The door opened before Ensign Jerusha Ericson, and she stepped into Temple Cole's cabin. The doctor smiled a greeting, but Jerusha saw that it was not a full smile.

"Yes, what is it, Ensign?" Her voice lacked warmth as well.

"Oh, nothing's wrong with me," Jerusha said. "I've had all my shots and such. I just wanted—well, I thought you might like to talk. I never get to see you anymore, Dr. Cole."

She saw the surgeon sizing up her visitor. Perhaps she was considering telling Jerusha to mind her own business. But then, maybe she *was* lonely. She had kept much to herself on this voyage.

"Sit down," the doctor said. "Can I get you something to drink—something to eat?"

Jerusha remained standing. "I wouldn't mind something. Do you have anything different?"

"Well, we have some piea juice from the planet Natola."

"That sounds exotic enough. Do *you* like it?"

"I think a taste for it has to be cultivated, but you might as well start cultivating." Dr. Cole crossed to the cooler at the small wet bar, took out a curiously shaped crystal bottle, and carefully poured a colorless liquid into two small glasses. "It doesn't take much," she said. "Just sip it."

Jerusha took the glass and almost fearfully took a sip. Her eyes flew open. She gasped and said, "What *is* this?"

"It's the juice distilled from a flower, the piea flower. I think it takes something like ten thousand of them to make one glass such as you have now."

"Then it must be frightfully expensive."

"Well, it is, but I like it, so I'm willing to give up some other things to have it. Sit down, Ensign."

Jerusha sat on one of the round, velvet seats. The chair was automatically controlled and formed itself to her body, almost like a caress. She laughed nervously. "These things always scare me. It seems the chair is trying to hug me."

"I know. I really prefer a chair like this one." Temple chose a firm chair covered with Durnoff leather.

Jerusha knew about Durnoff leather. It was so soft that it was almost like silk but was as durable as iron. It came from Durnoff oxen, a breed known to exist only on that particular planet.

Sipping her piea juice, the doctor asked, "Any word on the big, bad, red comet?"

"Just that it's getting closer. It worries me some."

"Oh, the captain will handle it."

Somehow, the way that Temple Cole said, "The captain," sent off alarm signals in Jerusha's head. She knew that Mark Edge had fallen hard for Temple Cole when she had first come aboard. She knew that the doctor had pretended interest in order to betray him. She also knew that when Dr. Cole deeply regretted aligning herself with the captain's enemies, she had been forgiven and restored as the *Daystar*'s medical officer. But today there seemed to be a . . . hardness? . . . in the physician. "Are you worried about something, Dr. Cole?" Jerusha asked abruptly.

"Isn't everybody?"

"I suppose so, but it helps sometimes to talk about it."

"Maybe you're right, Jerusha." Temple leaned back against her chair and closed her eyes. Her hair made little ringlets. It looked as if it was slightly damp from her shower. She ran her fingers through it in a gesture of frustration. "I haven't been feeling too well lately."

"Are you ill?"

"No, not physically." Suddenly she opened her eyes and said, "You don't know what happened to me, Jerusha. Before I came here to be the surgeon on the *Daystar*, I mean."

"No, not fully."

"It's not a nice story." A twisting of Temple Cole's lips showed that there was something not only hard but bitter inside her. Her voice was tinged with anger. "I fell in love with the captain of the ship I was serving on. He betrayed me. He almost lost the ship, and then at the hearing he laid it all at my door." She sipped again at the piea juice. "All the time they were reading the indictment against me, it seemed I could hear him saying, 'I love you, Temple.'"

Jerusha hardly knew how to answer. It was not her place, she felt, to counsel a woman several years older than she. Still, she managed to say, "It's hard to handle feelings of anger. I think that's about the hardest thing any of us have to do."

Temple shrugged. "I'm getting better at it. But it'll always be there."

"Both anger and the wish for revenge are hard to

47

deal with. Yet, Jesus said we're to forgive others as God has forgiven us."

"That man doesn't deserve forgiveness!" she snapped. "At least I'm certainly not ready to forgive him right now."

Jerusha held her tiny crystal glass in both hands and stared into the clear liquid. She was trying hard to think of some way to help this woman who obviously was having a very severe problem. After a pause, she decided what she must say.

"You know a lot about physical diseases, Dr. Cole. You probably know, as well, that there are some things that are as bad as a serious physical disease. I think one of them is bitterness. It eats away at us inside even as some diseases will devour and feed on the body."

The doctor gazed back at her. "I know that is true. Of course. I've thought about that many times," she said. "But there's nothing I can do about how I feel. I can't help my feelings."

"I . . . you know, sometimes I recite Scripture to myself, and one of my favorites is: 'Forgive us our debts, as we also have forgiven our debtors.'"

Doctor Cole stood to her feet, apparently disturbed by what she was hearing. "Well, I didn't mean to burden you with my problems," she said.

"Any time you want to talk, I'm available, Dr. Cole."

"Thank you, Ensign."

Jerusha sensed that she was being dismissed. She got up, too, and went to the door. But she turned back before she left. "You haven't seen the captain much lately."

"No."

The bare word told Jerusha a great deal, and she could not help feeling elated. She had been convinced for a long time that Temple Cole was not the woman for Capt. Mark Edge. "Well, you have been busy."

"Yes, I have. I have to see the captain soon, though. He hasn't been in to get his vitamin shot."

"He hates shots. I think he's really afraid of them," Jerusha said.

The ship's doctor laughed. "He's not afraid of a laser beam, but he's afraid to take a shot. We'll have to lure him into the dispensary, then. You can help me with that."

"I'll be glad to," Jerusha said.

She left the surgeon's quarters and strode down the corridor, feeling happier than she had in days. *She doesn't care for the captain,* she thought, *and I don't think he really cares for her either. It's best. They're just not suited for one another.*

The training room of the *Daystar* was more elaborate than one would have expected. It was Captain Edge's opinion that every member of the crew ought to be kept physically fit, and he had had the space enlarged so that now it was admirably suited to any sort of exercise.

Jerusha and Ringo had just finished their daily workout and were anxious to get back to their computer consoles. The red comet had many qualities that normal comets did not, and they were eager to continue their research.

As they cooled themselves down, Ringo was complaining. "This physical exercise thing is supposed to get us in better shape. The truth is, I feel worse than ever. My back is killing me." He began rubbing the small of his back.

Jerusha stopped bouncing up and down on the balls of her feet. "Come on, Ringo. You've said yourself

49

that you wish you could be as strong as Dai Bando. This exercise program is how you get there!"

"I know what I said, but I didn't think I'd be in this much pain." Ringo rubbed his back against the wall. "Jerusha, you're getting to be just like Jaleel. You don't have to throw me to the mat every chance you get! Lighten up."

Jerusha picked up her sweatshirt and quickly pulled it on over her shoulders. Tara Jaleel had ordered that each person using the exercise room must be dressed in the Jain Jayati training garment, a one-piece white outfit tied at the waist with a blue cloth belt. The sleeves and pant legs billowed out to allow maximum movement. Jerusha thought the outfit was cumbersome and drafty, and she attempted to wear her oversized sweatshirt whenever she could.

"Ringo, I'm not going to lighten up. Would you rather have Jaleel throwing you all over the room?"

"No, thank you very much! I just hurt all over, and it doesn't seem to matter to anyone that I do." Ringo stood looking around the exercise room. "Just look at this place. Every time I come in, Jaleel has made it look more and more like one of those martial arts places." Pointing his finger to the wall on their left, he continued. "Now she's got swords and axes mounted on the walls. And look there, Jerusha. She's painted a picture of that Shiva character right on the wall. It looks disgusting!"

Jerusha sighed. "I know, Ringo. I've been trying to get Captain Edge to listen to me, but he just doesn't want to hear any complaints about Jaleel. He wants us all in shape—says he doesn't want to hear any more fussing from us. He says he's doing it for our own good." Jerusha studied the painting of the god Shiva. "I'm going to have a good talk with Bronwen about this, though. It's one thing for Jaleel to idolize Shiva, but I don't think she should be able to push Shiva on the rest of us." Jerusha strolled out of the exercise room with a purposeful bounce to her walk.

Ringo stood looking at the painting of Shiva. Strangely, something about the picture attracted him—something he couldn't quite identify. In his mind, he suddenly pictured himself stronger and more muscular than even Dai Bando. He imagined himself inside a powerful, brawny body, not afraid of anything, and he smiled at the thought of finally being able to attract Raina St. Clair.

He thought, *If Lieutenant Jaleel's Jain Jayati program can help me get Raina—then it's worth it!* Ringo limped out of the training room, rubbing the small of his back with his right hand.

In appearance, Tara Jaleel, aged twenty-four, was perhaps the most unusual security officer on any starship. She was almost six feet tall and was as muscular and firm as training and diet could make her. She was a descendant of an old African tribe, the Masai. Masai warriors, if historical accounts were accurate, had produced the most courageous and fierce fighters on the continent of Africa.

Her features were attractive. She had a straight nose, a wide mouth, and large dark eyes. Her cheekbones were high, and her hair was short and curled close to her skull. People said that something about the way she moved reminded them of a large cat. And no one on the *Daystar* could endure a bout with her without paying the price in sore bones and bruised flesh.

No one, that is, except for Dai Bando.

The security officer always tried so hard to win. At

every encounter with Dai she put forth her full strength, something she could never do with anyone else aboard ship. If she had, there would have been a sick bay full of men and women with crushed bodies. Dai Bando was the one human being she had never been able to overcome.

And now Jaleel circled Dai once more, her hands lightly extended. She moved about the floor almost weightlessly. The boy seemed to float motionless before her. She started forward, and her hand flashed out. The heel of it was hardened almost to the texture of solid rock. It struck at his nose. If it had connected, in all probability it would have driven the bones up into his brain and killed him.

But Dai Bando's nose was not there. In a leisurely way, it seemed, he moved his head just a fraction so that Jaleel's blow missed by a quarter of an inch. He made no attempt to strike back, even though the force of the blow threw the weapons officer off balance.

With a grunt, she sprang back into a protective position. "You should have attacked then! When I was off balance!"

"I suppose so." Dai shrugged.

The boy claimed he didn't know where he got his tremendous strength and lightning reflexes. As a child, he said, he thought everyone had them, but he had quickly learned that others did not have his gift. Yet— in spite of his martial arts abilities—Jaleel had to acknowledge that there was a gentle spirit in the young Welshman.

His black hair fell over his forehead, and he looked very young as he circled her.

Jaleel suddenly launched a vicious kick at his stomach. He dodged back just enough so that her foot barely touched him, and he smiled. "You got me that time."

His cheerfulness enraged her. She knew that any other man would have been lying on the floor now in agony from that kick, but somehow Dai Bando seemed to be almost immune.

The two continued to circle each other, and Dai continued to avoid the lightninglike blows that she drove at him.

Suddenly the boy asked, "What do you believe, Lieutenant?"

"Believe about what?" A fine sheen of sweat had appeared on her face. Intent on the contest at hand, she kept her eyes locked on the young man in front of her.

"About Jai-Kando."

"It is the ancient martial arts that come from the Hindu Jain Jayati."

"Jain Jayati," Dai murmured. Then, as Jaleel once more launched herself at him, he leaped into the air, turned a full somersault over her head, and landed lightly on his feet behind her. He was waiting when she whirled around, furious, anger etched over her dark features. "What does Jain Jayati mean?"

"It means 'The believer who conquers.'"

This appeared to interest Dai Bando. "I like that. I think believers in Christ conquer, too."

"Bah! Christianity is a weak religion! I believe in Jainism."

"What exactly is that?"

Lieutenant Jaleel suddenly conceived a plan. *If I can just get his mind on what I'm saying, I can catch him off guard.* She smiled and lowered her hands but inched a little closer. "In my belief, the soul is reincarnated. We go through life after life until finally we reach perfection."

"I already understand that part. But what really

happens to a person? I mean, you're Lieutenant Tara Jaleel." A puzzled look came into Dai's eyes. "If you became somebody else in another life, you wouldn't be Lieutenant Jaleel."

"Eventually there will be no Lieutenant Jaleel."

"You mean you just vanish?"

"No! I will become part of a single, supreme being. The collection of the Perfected Liberated Souls."

Dai dropped his hands and stood without defense. "I don't think that's right, Lieutenant. It sounds like you'll become less and less and less. But the Bible teaches that we are always who we are. We become more and more. I wouldn't want to become less than I am right now. I don't see why you would."

Jaleel suddenly felt rage flash through her. She was a strong-minded woman. And she had killed before. With all her strength, Tara Jaleel threw herself at the boy slouching before her. In that split second, a thrill of excitement went through her, for she sensed he was not going to move.

I've got him this time! she thought exultantly. Her hand flashed forward. It touched his face.

But then she found her wrist grasped by a steely hand. She struck out with her other hand. This wrist too was pinned. She was held helpless.

Dai smiled into her eyes. "I really think you ought to reconsider, Lieutenant. It sounds like you're wanting to become part of a big bowl of stew."

"What are you talking about?" Jaleel gasped, her frustration growing—partly because of what the boy said but mostly because she could not free herself from his grasp.

"Well, I mean, you think everybody winds up as just one big collection. That's what happens to stew. Nobody would be anybody."

He released her then, and Jaleel glared at him, her eyes full of fury.

"That's all for this lesson!"

"All right, Lieutenant. Thanks a lot."

Jaleel watched Dai Bando walk away. When he was out of the training room, she whirled and went directly to a small chest mounted on the wall. She opened it with trembling fingers and looked at the image of the god Shiva within.

"I hate him!" she cried. "I hate him! Help me to overcome him!" she prayed. The metal idol looked back at her with a malevolent stare.

As Dai walked out of the training area toward the showers, he was more puzzled than ever about the weapons officer. *She's always angry,* he thought. *I'd sure like to see her become a Christian. If anybody on this ship needs the Lord, it's Lieutenant Jaleel.*

5

Barbie Dolls

Ringo programmed the pea-sized earplug by using the sharp end of a pin. Then he stuck the device into his ear and started down the corridor. The music began at once, and he moved his head from side to side in time with the beat. It was a new musical group that employed glass drums, which produced a ringing instead of the ordinary drumbeat. He liked the sound.

He halted at Mei-Lani Lao's cabin door and pushed the button. Immediately the door opened. It always fascinated him to see these door hatches work. The hatch mechanism began simply with a small slit about four feet high, then it opened into a larger circle, and finally it disappeared completely.

Stepping inside, Ringo saw his friend Mei-Lani sitting in front of a white enamel desk. He waved a greeting and walked over to her. "What's that you've got there?" he asked curiously.

Mei-Lani smiled shyly up at him. He'd always admired her beautiful almond-shaped eyes, and her hair was so black it almost seemed purple. She was off duty now, and instead of having her hair tightly braided around her head, it lay along her back in shiny, ebony waves.

"It's an old CD player, Ringo."

"What's that?"

"It plays music on a disk like this. See?" Mei-Lani held up a metallic disk four inches wide. It appeared to be made of aluminum.

Intrigued, Ringo took the disk from her. He rolled it over and stared at both sides. "Never saw one of these. Looks like it must be pretty old."

"Oh, yes. Computer disks like this were invented back on Earth a long, long time ago. About 1980, I think."

"How does it work?"

"Well, this player used to run on batteries." She flipped open the back and exposed the batteries, which said "Eveready" on the label. "Of course they don't work anymore."

"My, they're huge!" He pulled the Audio-ROM out of his ear and said, "The batteries to this one are built in, and it's tiny enough to put right in your ear." Ringo scrutinized Mei-Lani's old CD disk again and laughed. "Bet my Audio-ROM can hold a hundred times more music than this thing!"

"Well, they didn't have the technology for all that back in the twentieth century." She put the disk into the player and then turned it on. "See, it has a modern earphone that's wired to it. I've been listening to some of the old songs."

Inquisitive, Ringo put the plug in his left ear and took the other out. He listened for a moment, and his eyes widened. "I never heard stuff like this. What *is* it?"

"Oh, it's called rap music."

"Rap music? What does that mean? Do you rap somebody on the head while you're listening?"

Mei-Lani giggled and looked even younger than her thirteen years. Today she was wearing a simple silk dress with large crimson flowers on it, and her feet were clad with very basic sandals. "No. No. In those days, to rap with someone meant to talk with him, so some of the musical groups started talking their words instead of singing."

Ringo listened for a while longer, then grinned and pulled out the earpiece. "I guess I'll stick with the glass drums. That's my thing."

Mei-Lani took back the speaker and placed it on the table. "Glass drums are the in thing now, but that'll change. Taste in music changes so quickly." She pushed the CD player to one side. "Sit down and talk a while, Ringo, if you're not busy."

"I'm not." While he sat, Mei-Lani got up and took two glass containers out of the cooler. She brought them over. "Here, have a bottle of root beer."

"Oh, thanks! I sure like that stuff. It's hard to find nowadays."

"They drank a lot of root beer back in the old days, too. I made this root beer myself."

"You *make* root beer?"

"It's not too hard," she said.

Ringo marveled at her. She was actually a very talented girl. Reserved and shy, she constantly read and scanned old films to learn about the past.

Now Mei-Lani removed the top from her glass bottle and took a sip. "You know what I *really* like to do, Ringo?"

He grinned. "Yeah, you like to read, and study, and paint, and collect things."

She smiled at him. "You know me too well, but there's one thing you don't know." She put down the drink and crossed to another part of the room. Bending over, she opened a cabinet and pulled out a large box, which she brought back and set on the table. "I have this old collection. When I want to relax, here's what I really like, Ringo." She opened the box, and he bent over and peered into it.

"Well, look at that—it's dolls! But I never saw any dolls like this before."

"They used to be called Barbie dolls. Do you like them?"

Ringo reached into the box and picked up two. One was a long-legged young lady wearing a pair of white shorts and a halter. The other was a blond male doll. He had on a pair of blue jeans and a colorful shirt. "Well, one thing is for sure," Ringo said. "There never were any people as good-looking as these are. Not even in the olden days, I'll bet."

"That's true. They're idealized, but that's what kids wanted back in that period of time."

"I never could figure out what girls did with their dolls," Ringo confessed. "I mean, besides look at them."

"Oh, you give them names. This is Barbie, and this is Ken." She picked up two more, obviously much younger, and said, "This is Mike, and this is Sheree."

"How many of these things do you have?"

"Not many here. Back at home I've got about a hundred of them."

"A hundred!" Ringo was amazed. "They must have cost a fortune! Dolls like this are museum pieces today."

"Oh, they are antiques all right, but you can still find them, and I don't spend money for much of anything else."

"But what do you do with them, Mei-Lani?"

"You make clothes for them, and then you change their clothes, and then you act out things with them. You can create whole families with uncles and aunts and cousins and grandparents. Ken goes out with Barbie, and then they date other people." Her eyes sparkled, and she said, "Don't tell anybody about this. They'll think I'm crazy, playing with dolls at my age."

"Sounds like more fun than some of the things that I do."

Ringo was basically an unhappy boy. He had been raised in a state orphanage. Around his neck he wore a medallion, hidden by his uniform. It had a falcon on one side. On the other side was the profile of a strong-looking man and words in an unknown language—one that even Mei-Lani had not been able to decode, although she was good at languages.

Mei-Lani took up a Barbie doll and began to put a beautiful crimson dress on it. Suddenly she said, "Are you worried about something, Ringo? You are, aren't you?"

"Me? No. Why do you ask that?"

"I don't know. You just seem troubled somehow."

Ringo desperately wanted to tell Mei-Lani that he *was* worried. He wanted to tell her he was unhappy. He wanted to tell her about how he was falling in love with Raina St. Clair but that she liked Dai Bando. He did not know how to start.

And then Mei-Lani looked straight at him and said, "You like Raina, don't you?"

Ringo gaped at her. "Are you a mind reader?"

Mei-Lani placed two tiny slippers on the feet of the doll. Then she tilted her head to one side and looked up at Ringo seriously. "You don't have to be a mind reader to know that, Ringo. I can tell just by the way you look at her. And I know something else. You're jealous of Dai."

"Well, that's not true!"

Mei-Lani didn't argue but said no more on the subject.

Ringo was glad. He was too uncomfortable to talk right now. And he guessed that since she was a sensitive girl, she knew better than to press the point.

Ringo stayed for twenty minutes longer, for he enjoyed Mei-Lani's company. He felt safe with her, which meant he knew she was not judging him. He'd always felt that he was the weakest, the most incapable of all the Rangers. Mei-Lani, however, was so mild and sweet that he didn't have this feeling when he was around her.

But finally he got up. "Well, I've got to go to work. If that red comet gets any closer, we're not gonna have any computers left."

"It sounds bad."

"It is bad. If the computers shut down on this ship, we'll go crashing into the first meteorite that happens along. Computers run the guidance system and just about everything else. Yeah, it's something to worry about. I think I better go check and see if everything's all right."

"Come back when you get through, Ringo. We can listen to some rap music, and maybe I'll make some of those little cakes you like so much."

Mei-Lani had a tiny oven in her cabin. Ringo remembered the delicious small cakes she baked. And she brewed a very fine variety of tea that he had learned to enjoy.

"All right," he said. "I will."

Captain Edge stood beside Bronwen Llewellen before the view screen as both of them looked at the planet they were approaching, Ciephus.

"As far as I can tell from photographs," Edge said, "the place is completely uninhabited today, except for that one city."

Bronwen replied, "Ciephus is a very arid planet, Captain—no oceans, rivers, or lakes." Looking over the dull brown and purple landscape, she pointed out four locations on the planet's surface. "Four cities were built on the only known water reserves on Ciephus.

Three of the cities were abandoned long ago. Their water table reserves ran dry. This city located in the southeast quadrant"—Llewellen indicated the place with her pointer—"is the only one left with a water supply. Data confirms that this town too will run out of water very soon. Our records indicate that its name is Tyrian. Probably a very practical name for the city, I think, judging by the purple hue of the soil the town sits on."

Captain Edge pondered the planet displayed on the screen. It roughly reminded him of Mars, except without the "canals."

"Bring magnification up fifty percent on Tyrian," he ordered.

As Edge and the navigator watched, the magnification lenses brought Tyrian into better view.

"It certainly doesn't look like your typical desert metropolis," Bronwen remarked thoughtfully. "Most of the buildings seem very small. They appear to be made out of some sandlike material."

The captain studied the city. "But see that large structure in the center of the city—it appears very different from the buildings around it." Edge bent over the viewer and looked at the building more closely. "The construction looks . . . metallic? And it must be two hundred feet taller than anything else."

The viewer was filling with static.

Edge rubbed his right wrist. "Bronwen, do you have any idea how the red comet will affect Ciephus? Is there any other planet we can make it to? Any more suitable place?" He didn't like the idea of being stranded on a planet with limited water.

"I believe we're going to have to land here, Captain," Bronwen said after some thought.

"I hate to put the *Daystar* down, but if that comet

knocks out all our computers and navigational instruments, we'll be in big trouble."

"I think, then, we'd better land near Tyrian. After the comet has passed us by, it'll be safe to take off again."

A tiny pinging sound caught Edge's attention, and he touched the radio on his belt. "Edge here!"

"Ensign Jordan, Captain."

"What is it, Jordan?"

"The tri-star gravitational pull of the Orion belt has done just what I thought it would do."

"What's that?"

"It's pulled the comet in our direction, and it's moving much faster now."

"When did that happen?"

"Just now. We first detected the red comet as it was exiting the Lepus Constellation. Long-range scanners projected that the comet heading vectored with Betelgeuse. Now computer data shows that a quirk in the Orion Belt gravitational field has influenced the comet and turned its heading toward Orion's belt." Heck paused for breath, then continued. "The comet will either collide with this planet, or it will be a near miss. Right now, it looks too close to call. Computer systems are becoming more inaccurate, so it is hard to be precise."

"All right, Jordan. Edge out." He turned back to Bronwen and made up his mind. "That's it. We'll have to land and warn the inhabitants that they're going to be brushed by a comet. I just hope it doesn't hit head-on."

"So do I. That would be bad for all of us."

The *Daystar* made a smooth flight approach to the city of Tyrian. During the landing procedures, Zeno

Thrax stood at the captain's side, alert and ready for trouble as the ship came in for a landing. "It's a good thing that all these flat plains are here, Captain."

"You're right there, Zeno." Edge looked over to the mountains that surrounded the horizon. "We couldn't land in those."

"No, sir. But you did make a fine landing."

"Sir!" Tara Jaleel hurried up to the captain. "There's movement outside."

Edge went to a porthole and saw what she had seen. "It's people, all right. They're coming out from the city to greet us."

"We'd better take security precautions, sir."

"Minimum security," Edge said quickly. He knew Tara Jaleel was quick with the weapons, and he saw the frown that appeared on her face.

"We don't know how dangerous these people are," she protested.

"From what I can see," Bronwen Llewellen said, "they don't look dangerous at all." She was peering out the port with a small set of binoculars. "But there are a lot of them."

"Captain, we'd better have armed security. We don't know anything about these people," Jaleel insisted.

"Go ahead," Edge agreed reluctantly. He knew from experience that innocent-looking things could turn out to be deadly. He himself had been badly burned once when he had trusted just such innocent appearance.

The entire *Daystar* crew was jostling about the portholes. Even the dog was there. Jerusha nudged her and said, "Get away, Contessa!" The German shepherd whined and backed off, looking mournfully up at her friend.

"Look at this, Dai," Raina said.

Dai Bando pressed his face next to hers as they peered out the porthole. "I never saw such a welcoming committee. There must be hundreds of them."

Ringo was looking for an unused porthole when he saw Dai standing beside Raina, their faces cheek-to-cheek, looking out the tiny window. His jaw hardened, and he kept going. He joined Temple Cole, the surgeon, at her porthole and said, "Hello, Dr. Cole. Interesting view out there?"

"Why, hello, Ringo." The doctor was wearing a silver colored smock over her sky blue uniform today, and she looked very fresh and even excited. "Have a look. Did you ever see anything like that?"

Ringo looked out. Most of the people were quite small, he saw—not more than four or five feet tall. As they crowded closer to the spacecraft, he commented that they were very young looking as well. "I think they are all children!"

"They appear to be. And look at their complexions," Dr. Cole murmured. "I've never seen a complexion quite like that. It's rather like a bad sunburn, but surely that's not it. Not for all of them."

"And look how ragged their clothes are! They look like they're all wearing shorts and old T-shirts."

"I'm wondering where the adults are," Temple said thoughtfully.

Ringo stared harder through the port. "Maybe hiding where we can't see them. Getting ready to attack us. Or they could be afraid of us!" he guessed.

Dr. Cole studied the crimson children. "But the *children* aren't afraid, Ringo. I've seen scared kids before, and I don't see fear in these boys and girls at all. The look on their faces reminds me of . . . something, though. Something from long ago . . ."

"Well, where do *you* think the adults are?"

"Maybe they're dead. I don't know. I hope not! One thing I do know—these children look undernourished." The doctor put her hands on her hips. "I have a bad feeling about this."

Ringo didn't answer. He had never seen so many children who looked so similar and so hopeless. He found himself thinking, *Whatever it is you guys need, we're here to help.*

As Ringo turned away from the port, Contessa jumped up on her hind legs and looked out. She sniffed around the window. Unable to smell anything through the glass, she dropped down and ran for the *Daystar*'s exit ramp.

Captain Edge had asked Jerusha to join him and Tara Jaleel in a conference up on the bridge. Lieutenant Jaleel was testy and irritable. She spent several minutes trying to convince Edge to let her go out and recon the area.

"No," Edge said for the third time, "we don't have time for this! That comet is going to be here soon! I don't think we'll be in any danger from these *children*, Lieutenant Jaleel. They look harmless."

"Things aren't always what they seem!"

Jerusha glanced at the older woman and saw the anger in her eyes.

About that time Heck came onto the bridge with a report for the captain. Then he looked beyond Edge to the scene outside, and his eyes grew bright. "Hey," he said, "maybe there's treasure in that city, and they'll give it to us for telling them about the comet!"

Edge glared at his electronics expert. "Don't you ever think of anything but money and profit?"

"Sure. I think about eating, and music, and dancing, and having a good time."

Edge could not help but grin at the boy. "I'm afraid that's all I thought about when I was your age."

"You mean you don't think about partying and stuff like that anymore?"

Jerusha, listening, suspected that the captain had allowed too much leniency.

"Never mind what I think," Edge said. "But I'm telling you, Heck, hustling is a mighty poor lifestyle, and that's what you're headed for."

Jerusha said quietly, "Heck, the person who loves silver will never be satisfied with silver. The Bible says that."

"What does that mean?" Heck was wearing his uniform, but, as usual, he had added to it. Being completely color-blind, he could not tell what he was wearing, which was actually a purple neckerchief and a brilliant yellow-orange belt. It almost hurt Jerusha's eyes to look at him, the colors were so glaringly ill suited.

"It means," she said, "that the people who love money won't ever get enough of it. You could give them enough gold and silver to load the world, and they'd still want more."

"That's what I want," Heck said instantly.

"You want what?" Edge asked.

"More!"

Jerusha threw up her hands. "I give up," she said. "You're totally hopeless."

She turned to the porthole and looked out at the red-complexioned little people swarming about the ship. "Well," she murmured quietly, "it'll be interesting to see what they have to say about us—and the red comet."

6

The Children of Tyrian

Tara Jaleel fingered her Neuromag pistol, and her eyes whipped this way and that as she stepped outside the *Daystar*. She had insisted on going first, for she was by nature suspicious and aggressive. Moving down the ramp that connected the door of the cruiser to the ground, she was followed closely by Captain Edge, who was in turn trailed by Mei-Lani Lao and Jerusha.

Jerusha was glad she had been chosen. Edge had said he wanted the two girls along because Jerusha was highly sensitive to people and because Mei-Lani was an expert historian and linguist.

Jaleel halted, and the others came up beside her. Her gaze swept the crowd that advanced quickly toward them, and she said, "I don't like this, Captain."

"They still seem harmless enough to me," Edge said. "They're so small, and they all look so *young.*"

"That may be from some effect of this planet!" Jaleel exclaimed. "For all we know, they may be a hundred years old or more!"

Edge turned to Mei-Lani. "Can you try to see what language they speak?"

Mei-Lani walked toward the crowd of native children, and several immediately pushed close to her. All wore ragged clothing, and all had the same reddish, sunburned appearance.

Mei-Lani spoke a phrase in one language. There was no response. Quickly she tried a series of languages. Finally, in despair, she turned back to Captain Edge. "They don't seem to understand *any* of the more common languages of the galaxy."

"They may understand more than you think," Tara Jaleel said grimly.

Studying the small people, Mei-Lani said thoughtfully, "I just had a thought, Captain."

"What is it?"

"Back on Earth there used to be some hard times, and I remember seeing old motion pictures of starving children standing around with empty expressions just like this."

"I've seen some of those, too, Mei-Lani," Jerusha said. "These boys and girls remind me of . . ." Suddenly she was certain there was no harm meant to them by these pathetic specimens. She reached out a hand, and a boy immediately took it. He was thin, and his eyes held a longing in them that Jerusha could not identify but only pity.

There had been times of war on Earth, Jerusha knew, when children were abandoned and, as a result, nearly starved. "Look how thin they are," she said. "And look at their eyes."

Edge appeared baffled. Jerusha sensed that he had a bad feeling about the whole situation. He had landed before on alien planets where there were monstrous creatures to face, but now they were looking around at a swarm of small, underfed, and ragged boys and girls. "I truly don't know how best to handle this," he said.

"Maybe you ought to call Dr. Cole," Mei-Lani suggested. "If she could examine some of these youngsters, she might tell us more."

"You don't know that they're *young*," Jaleel insisted.

"Of course, they're young," Jerusha put in. "Look

at them. They're just like any other children except for that strange, red color."

"There's something wrong here," Jaleel insisted doggedly. "Where are the adults?"

"That's what's got me worried," Edge said. "Children like this couldn't run a city or anything else."

More red-complexioned youngsters gathered close around, staring out of large eyes.

The captain said, "We're going to have to go into the city and see what's there."

"Don't you go in, Captain," Jaleel said. "Let me go."

"No, actually I think I'll send Dai Bando. He's the quickest and the best able to take care of himself."

At these words Jaleel drew herself up, and her eyes flashed with anger, but she said nothing.

"Dai!" Edge called out, and the boy, who had been watching from the door of the spaceship, ran down the ramp and jogged toward the captain. "I want you to go into the city and have a quick look around."

"Yes sir."

"But be careful. You don't know what's in there. Something about this situation gives me the creeps."

"I'll be careful, Captain."

Dai trotted off at once, and Jerusha thought, *He runs like a deer!* She watched until he was just a small figure in the distance.

"Mei-Lani," Edge said, "why don't you try to communicate again with these people—if you can think of some way you haven't already tried."

"I'll try, sir."

But no matter how many dialects she tried, the children seemed absolutely unable to understand her.

Suddenly Jerusha said, "Sir, I think they're hungry."

"Well, they look like it. Maybe we ought to offer them something to eat."

"I think that would be a good idea, Captain," Jerusha said. "Let me go to the galley and put something together."

"Go ahead. We might as well be doing something useful while we're waiting on Dai to get back."

"Yes sir. And I'll be quick." Jerusha turned and ran to the ship.

In the galley, the head cook, a woman named Pearl Gates, listened as Jerusha excitedly told her what was needed. The cook was a tall, rawboned woman. She was always called "Pearly Gates."

Then Pearly said, "How am I supposed to know what they eat? They're aliens of some kind, aren't they?"

"They look just like hungry children to me."

"No, I saw them out the porthole, Jerusha. They're red! Redder than normal people!"

"But I don't think that has anything to do with their being hungry," Jerusha argued. "Please, Pearly, just throw together anything you've got here."

"All right. I'll do my best. You'll have to help me, though."

The two quickly went to work. They set out food that required little preparation. It consisted of sandwiches and chips of different sorts and portions of several leftover cakes. They filled two large trays.

"This will do just fine, Pearly. Help me carry it out, will you?"

"All right, but I don't want to get close to none of those red things."

"Pearly put together a nice snack, Captain," Jerusha announced when they were outside.

"Fine. Start giving it out."

"I'll help," Mei-Lani said.

The girls began passing out sandwiches. Even Pearly

decided to help. Tara Jaleel stood rigidly by, refusing to have anything to do with the food distribution.

Jerusha handed a sandwich to one of the rosy-hued children, saying, "Here. Eat this. It'll be good."

The girl, who was no more than six or seven, Jerusha estimated, shyly smiled, reached out, and took the sandwich. She took a bite, ravenously devoured the entire sandwich, then held out her hands for more.

"Why, they're starving, Captain!" Mei-Lani exclaimed.

All the children pushed in close then, and the girls and Pearly handed out the food until it was gone.

"I don't know what this is all about," Edge said, "but it's not good where you have starving children. Dish up some more grub, Pearly. See that they get enough. And they need something to drink too."

Twice, Jerusha and Mei-Lani, now led by Pearly Gates, brought out food, and finally the children seemed satisfied. They still had not spoken, but their delight at being fed was obvious.

Then Jerusha looked across the flat plain and saw Dai Bando running back. "Here comes Dai!" she called.

"He flies like an Olympic runner," Mei-Lani said.

"Yes, he could make a fortune as a professional athlete," Edge said enviously. "I never could run like that when I was his age."

Dai loped across the open plain and ran up to Captain Edge, not even breathing hard. "Sir, it's a *strange* place."

"Did you see anything suspicious?" Jaleel spoke before the captain could. "Any guns? Any lasers?"

"No, I didn't see anything like that," Dai said.

"You wouldn't even know what to look for," Jaleel sneered. Turning to the captain, she said, "Let me go and check things out."

"We'll all go in," Edge said. "Did you see any adults, Dai? Any grown people at all?"

"No sir. Just some children like these. There's a big building in the center of the city, but there's no one in it, except some children, of course."

Edge made up his mind. "All right. We all go in for a recon." He looked back to where Zeno Thrax stood by the cruiser. "Number One, you're in charge until I get back."

"I'd like to go with you, sir," Thrax said.

"No, better not. If anything happens to us, get the ship out of here. And no rescue attempts, you understand?"

Thrax nodded slowly. "Yes sir. I understand."

"Come on," Edge said. "We'll have a closer look."

Cautiously, the group moved across the dry plain toward the town, while some of the children trailed behind. When they reached the gates and entered, Jerusha said, "Why, the town is falling apart! I never saw such a run-down place!"

"Something's certainly wrong about this," Edge said. "Nobody's taken care of any of the buildings. And yet people obviously live here. Or lived here."

As they wandered along the street that Edge thought headed to the town's center, Jerusha pointed out to him the huge heaps of leaves and trash that littered the road and actually flowed into the open doors of some of the houses. Many glass panes had been broken out of the windows, and wild vines had their way with other buildings—literally covering them.

And then they came to what seemed to be the center of the city. Here were many empty shops whose front windows had been broken into thousands of pieces of glass that sparkled on the ground. Ahead stood an enormous metallic building.

"There's the building I was telling you about, Captain," Dai Bando said. "It looks to be the biggest one in the city."

"Pretty strange-looking structure. It looks kind of streamlined for this place. Almost like a spaceship—if you use your imagination." Edge responded thoughtfully.

They went inside, followed by curious children. Jaleel had her hand weapon out. Her eyes were darting everywhere. The Space Rangers, led by Edge, began to check out room after room for people. However, they found no one.

They did soon make one startling discovery.

Mei-Lani said, "Sir, have you noticed all the clothing lying around?"

"Yes, I certainly have," Edge replied. "And I don't understand it."

They were standing in the middle of a huge conference room, and on the chairs and tables and on the floor were piles of clothing, including shoes.

"I don't understand this at all," Edge said. "It's as if a lot of people just changed clothes." He picked up a tunic. "This would never fit any of these kids around here. It would take a big man to fill this out." He glanced around the large room. "I don't like this," he muttered under his breath, and he shivered slightly as though an eerie feeling gripped him. "I don't like it at all."

"I don't like it either, sir," Jerusha said, stepping closer to him. "There's something wrong here. Dreadfully wrong."

Edge looked down at her and then nodded grimly. "Then it's our job, Ensign Ericson, to find out what it is."

7
Where Are the Big People?

Raina St. Clair walked around among the boys and girls who had stayed by the *Daystar.* Everyone on the crew knew by now that something was dreadfully wrong with this planet—and with the city in the distance. She glanced toward it now, wondering how the recon party was doing.

But Raina was on a mission. Dr. Cole had called her aside a few minutes ago, saying, "Raina, we need to examine some of these children. I understand that no one's been able to communicate with them."

"No, Dr. Cole, not even Mei-Lani, and you know how good she is at languages."

"Well, it's important that I get one of them into the sick bay. Will you go outside and try to win the confidence of one of them? We could have a security team bring one in by force, but I'd rather not do that."

"Oh, no," Raina said. "I hope that won't be necessary. Let me try."

Now, as she moved among the children, she thought, *Which child shall I choose? A boy or a girl? Younger or older?* She noted that one child especially, a girl and seemingly curious, was staying very close to her. She turned and smiled down at her, and for a moment she thought she saw a flicker of emotion in the child's eyes.

"Hello. My name is Raina," she said, pointing to her chest. She waited for a response, but there was none. Finally, she decided to take a chance.

She reached out her hand and was delighted when the girl immediately took it. Smiling again, Raina said slowly, "Come with me, please. We want you to see the inside of the ship." Again there was no response, but when Raina started toward the cruiser, the child allowed herself to be led.

"That's right." Raina kept smiling her encouragement. Then she reached into her pocket, pulled out a piece of candy, and handed it to the girl. With her free hand the child immediately took the sweet and put it into her mouth. Her eyes were on Raina all the time. She was no more than eight or nine. She had large, pale blue eyes and thick brown hair. But the hair was not combed, and the child was absolutely filthy.

"I'd like to give you a bath and fix your hair," Raina murmured. "Maybe I will. Just come. That's right."

Remarkably, the child allowed Raina to walk her up the ramp into the ship.

Raina was afraid that, once inside, the girl would be intimidated, but she merely looked around with curiosity, then back toward Raina. "Do you like it in here? Come along. I want you to meet Dr. Cole." She led the girl down the corridor until she reached the sick bay, where Dr. Cole stood waiting with anxiety in her eyes.

"Did you have any trouble, Raina?"

"No, it was wonderfully easy. She's a sweet child, really." Reaching into her pocket, she produced another piece of candy, saying, "This is for you. And this is Dr. Cole."

The little girl looked at the doctor, but Raina saw no trace of fear in her.

Temple Cole gently brushed the girl's dirty hair back from her forehead. She smiled at her, saying, "I wish I knew your name, but since there doesn't seem to be any way to find that out, we'll just have to get along without it."

Raina said, "There's something so pathetic about this. I wonder if they can even communicate with each other!"

"I'm sure they must be able to do that, at least. I don't see how they could have survived without language." She patted the leather cushion of an elevated bed and said, "Would you mind getting up here, sweetheart?" Cole looked from the child's eyes to the bed and back again.

To Raina's surprise, the girl seemed to understand what the doctor wanted. Going to the bed, she stepped up on a small stool and seated herself. Then she looked expectantly at them.

"I hope these tests don't frighten her. If you have any more of that candy, you might feed it to her, one at a time."

"What sort of tests are you going to do, Doctor?"

"Oh, none that will hurt! It used to be that we had to extract DNA samples from hair, skin, blood, and other tissues. Now we have this!" Dr. Cole held up a small device that looked very similar to an ordinary checkerboard piece, except that it was blue with silver veins running through it. "It's called a Pyramidal Extrapolator."

She handed the little instrument to Raina, who examined it and then gave it back to the doctor.

"How does it work?" Raina asked softly, not wanting to alarm the child sitting on the bed next to her.

"It's a much more common device than you think. They actually use one kind of these for security purposes—on doors, for example. Those look different from this one, but they work somewhat on the same principle."

"Dr. Cole, how does *this* one work?" Raina's voice was a little louder.

"This is able to measure DNA strands located in the two large bundles of motor fibers from the cerebral cortex that reach the medulla oblongata and are continuous with the pyramidal tracts of the spinal cord."

The ensign suspected that she had a glazed look in her eyes. The doctor certainly knew that Raina St. Clair didn't understand what she was explaining.

"Raina, let's just say that I put the DNA gizmo on your neck, and then it will tell the medical computer tons of stuff we want to know. Everyone's DNA is unique. Nobody has DNA like yours. DNA is similar in many ways, but no two people have identical DNA."

Dr. Cole gently placed the instrument on the back of the child's neck.

The child's large eyes looked toward Raina, and Raina smiled at her reassuringly.

After a couple of minutes, the doctor carried the unit over to her computer and placed the device in a slot. The computer screen began to display information.

The crimson child watched Dr. Cole. Then she turned her head toward Raina again. Her eyes warmed as Raina spoke soft, comforting words to her.

Dr. Cole worked efficiently and quickly, while Raina occupied herself with smiling at the girl and giving her candy from time to time. Finally Temple nodded with satisfaction. "Well, that's all I'll need."

"What did you find out?"

"I found out that she *is* a child. Now if you'll go out and get at least two more, we'll have enough to confirm that this one isn't an isolated instance."

Raina and the child went down the cruiser ramp. With the little girl at her side, she had no trouble getting two volunteers. This time she chose one of the larger children, a boy who appeared to be nearly sixteen and an older girl.

As they readily accompanied Raina into the ship, she thought, *I believe I could have gotten any of them to come. They're so anxious to please. Maybe it's just hunger, but somehow I think it's more than that. They're lonesome!*

None of the three sample children responded to language. They did respond to gestures and to the expressions on the faces of the Earth people.

After Dr. Cole had tested the two new children, Raina said, "Dr. Cole, there's something *awful* about this, but I don't know what. I just don't understand it."

Dr. Cole bobbed her head, sending her strawberry curls into a slight bouncing motion. She was accustomed to difficult situations, as most physicians are—Raina knew that. But her violet eyes were troubled as she said quietly, "It would bother anyone. Something strange lies behind all of this. I don't know whether I'm more afraid for Captain Edge to find out *why* this is going on—or if he doesn't find out anything."

The building to which Capt. Mark Edge returned his recon team was unusual indeed. Although most of the other buildings were covered with wild vines, this metallic central structure had none.

They stood again at its wide, solid doors, and Edge tapped the metal exterior. "This is baffling. Remember the old *Daystar?*" When everyone nodded, he said, "Sections of that ship were very old, especially the fuselage. There wasn't a square inch of that cruiser that I didn't know. And the skin of this building feels like the skin of the old *Daystar* fuselage!"

"What does that mean, Captain?" Mei-Lani asked.

Edge frowned at the interior walls as they went back inside. "The Hydrogen Effect," he said.

Jerusha picked up on Captain Edge's explanation. "Mei-Lani, when a starship travels through space, it has a force field that protects it from being hit by meteorites, space debris, and lots of other stuff—"

"I already know that, but—"

"Mei-Lani . . ." Edge took back his explanation. "The force field traps hydrogen particles inside the field envelope. As the ship starts and stops, changes course, jumps to light speed, and so on, the hydrogen particles bounce off the outer skin of the ship. It's not dangerous, but after a few years, the skin of the ship has a very faint dimpling texture that you can feel with your fingertips—if you know what you're looking for."

On the recon team's initial exploration, Edge had decided that most of the structure consisted of living quarters. These circled the perimeter of the ship several stories high. As they walked the corridors again, he murmured, "And these are very basic living quarters at best."

On the first look through, they had done nothing but merely glance into every room, just looking for people. Edge decided they would explore the odd structure again, more thoroughly this time. The curious children had long ago wandered off.

They returned to the "conference room," and Captain Edge once again pondered the hundreds of outfits of clothing lying on chairs, tables, and floor.

The captain said, "My bet is that whatever happened to the adults of this city happened right here." Again he picked up a tunic and placed it across his chest. "This is definitely an adult shirt."

An adjoining room contained machinery of some sort. Jerusha looked upward and said to him, "Captain, have you noticed?—there are stadium-size *view screens* mounted just below the ceiling. And that bank of machinery over there—they look like a kind of computer, don't they?"

Captain Edge glanced up and grunted. He had been quietly staring at a palm-sized device on a wall shelf. He picked it up. It had strange markings on it, markings that were repeated on the bank of "computers"—if that was what they were.

"I've never seen anything like that," Jerusha said, peering at the instrument.

"Neither have I," Mei-Lani said. "What about you, Lieutenant?"

"You guys are the experts. You tell *me* what it is," she mocked, as she rubbed her hand along the intricate designs embedded in the computers' surface.

The metallic-looking boxes filled the nearby wall. They indeed resembled computer control and relay units. Mei-Lani and Jerusha walked over to examine the equipment more closely.

Jerusha waved her personal scanning unit all along the row of odd machines. "Nothing is working," she said. "The scanner doesn't pick up any energy readings from these." She indicated the metallic boxes. "Those things are probably computers, though. It looks like they're hooked up to that big contraption in the middle."

Edge studied the tall apparatus in the center of the room, thinking, *It must be one hundred feet tall and twenty-five feet in diameter.* The mechanism was built with translucent windows that showed thousands of swirling red lights swimming around in the gaseous substance that filled it.

Jerusha moved her scanner across the bottom of the central device. "Sir, there are energy readings coming from this mechanism—very faint electromagnetic fluctuations! I am also picking up some bioelectrical impulses that I can't localize. The red comet must be getting close. It is definitely affecting this scanner. Anyway, all this has me bewildered."

Jaleel sneered. "Imagine that! Blondie doesn't know everything, does she!" She laughed out loud.

"I'm afraid this is definitely outside my experience." Jerusha said defensively.

Edge puzzled over the swirling red lights visible through the small windows in the apparatus. "What *is* this thing?" he asked himself out loud. "And what are those red lights spiraling around inside of it?" The engravings located on the metal surface were extremely intricate. Edge scratched his chin, then took a few steps backward and shivered. "I don't know. I know it's not scientific, but this whole thing gives me the creeps."

"I know what you mean, Captain," Dai Bando said. He too shuddered slightly as he glanced about the computer room. "It's not natural. I'd rather be facing a physical enemy than stuff like this."

This time even Jaleel nodded in agreement.

Edge hesitated for a moment more, then touched the radio on his belt. "Captain Edge here. Calling Dr. Cole."

"Cole here, Captain. What have you found?"

"You first. What have *you* found? What about these people?"

"All these 'people,' as you call them, are indeed children. They're perfectly normal, except for their color and the fact that they don't understand any language that we can discover."

"You're sure they're children?"

"I know they are children. I tested their DNA. They're all exactly what they seem."

"Well, I don't know what to think, Temple. We're in

the middle of one of the buildings here, and there are machines that we can't even identify—machines with strange markings on them . . ."

"Doesn't Mei-Lani recognize any of them?"

"She says no, and it's likely she would if they were at all familiar in the galaxy."

"Anything else strange?"

"I'm afraid so. I don't know what it means, but in the building where we are now there are piles of clothes everywhere—shoes, underwear—everything. It makes no sense."

"What sort of clothes?"

"Just . . . garments. Nothing unusual about them that I can see—except they're all made for adults."

"Both men and women?"

"Yes. Now listen, Temple, I want you to send Raina, Ivan, and Jordan over here to the city."

"Do you want me to come, too?"

"Not right away. We won't stay here overnight. I'd like for those three to examine what we've found—and most of all to see if they can get these computers working. I'm not thinking too clearly. As a matter of fact, I'm pretty well at my wit's end."

"Don't let anything happen to you, Captain."

The personal message brought a little life into Captain Edge's face. "I'll be careful," he said. "In case I'm not here when they arrive, you tell the crew to watch themselves when they start probing this device in here. Whatever it is may be the thing that killed off the adult population."

"I'll warn them." There was a slight silence, and then Dr. Temple Cole said in a voice that was barely above a whisper, "Take care of yourself. I don't want anything to happen to you."

8

The Singer and the Song

Dai Bando watched patiently as Jerusha and Captain Edge and the others examined the contents of the large Tyrian conference room. He felt useless. Dai was not a student of science, but he thought that he ought to be doing something.

"Captain," he said, coming closer to where Edge was studying one of the computers, "would it be all right if I do a little more looking around the city?"

"Might be a good idea, Dai. Why don't you take Mei-Lani with you? I don't know what to tell you to look for. But if you find anything unusual, report back at once. And be careful!"

"Yes sir!" Dai glanced at Mei-Lani, who nodded agreeably and joined him.

Leaving the others to continue their investigations, Dai and Mei-Lani went outside and turned down the street to the right.

"I don't know what I'm looking for," Dai said. "I just felt like I wasn't doing any good in there."

"I felt the same way, Dai."

The two walked on, one and then the other commenting on the dilapidated aspect of the town. Buildings were scarred and beaten by time. The streets themselves were broken up. Weeds grew in the sidewalks. Vines crawled up over some of the lower portions of the buildings.

"It looks like a ghost town," Mei-Lani remarked.

"What's a ghost town? A town with ghosts in it? This place is spooky enough for that."

"No." Mei-Lani smiled. "Back in the old days in the American West, towns would sometimes be abandoned. People would just walk away and leave them and go elsewhere, so the towns would be empty. Truly a little spooky, I guess. So they would be called 'ghost towns.'"

"I wish I knew as much as you do about everything," Dai said wistfully. "No, I wish I knew one hundredth as much as you do. You're the smartest girl I ever saw, Mei-Lani."

Her cheeks flushed with pleasure at the compliment. She always acted embarrassed at compliments. "Oh, not really, Dai."

"Yes, you are. You know all about languages, and poets, and philosophers, and history. I don't know anything. I don't even know what I'm doing on this voyage! I guess the captain just needed a weak mind and a strong back."

"You don't have a weak mind! Don't say that!"

Surprised at Mei-Lani's emotion, Dai turned his head to look down at her. She was so small and delicate that he felt very protective of her. "Well, I *am* stupid."

"You are not stupid! I don't ever want to hear you say that again! If you do, I'll—" She raised her fist and pounded his right arm. "I'll take a switch to you!" she said.

Dai laughed. "I'll be careful then. I wouldn't want you to do that."

"I mean it, Dai. Stop putting yourself down."

"I'm just facing up to the truth," he said, surprised at the way this conversation was going. Even from the beginning of his service with the Space Rangers, he'd known that the others were all experts. "Well, look at us," he said. "Ringo's a computer genius, Heck knows everything about electronics, Raina is great at communications, and Jerusha's one of the best engineers in the fleet. And you are . . . well . . . just what I said. What can *I* do?"

"You once saved Raina's life because you are strong, for one thing."

"That's what I said—a strong back and a weak mind."

"Where's my switch?" Mei-Lani suddenly reached up and caught a handful of Dai's jet black hair. She pulled his head down and put her fist against his nose. "I wish I were strong enough. I'd punch you every time you say something like that. Don't you know what you do to yourself when you say bad things about yourself?"

"No. What do I do?"

"You start believing them."

"I read a book once—well, a part of one—that said you're supposed to tell yourself every day that you're great or wonderful or handsome. But I don't see how that *makes* anybody really great or wonderful or handsome."

"No, it doesn't work like that." Mei-Lani released his hair, then took his arm, saying, "Let's go on. We need to keep looking."

They walked for another fifty feet before she picked up the conversation. "We all have weaknesses, Dai, but we all have strengths too. Nothing's much worse than listening to someone who keeps talking about how great he is. That's pride, and the Bible says that's a sin God especially hates."

"He does?"

"The Bible says, 'There are six things which the Lord hates.' And the first one that it mentions is a proud look. God hates pride."

"Well, I'm all right then." Dai smiled. "You really think it's not good to talk about your failures?"

"It means you're comparing yourself with other people! And God has made us all different. He didn't make a hummingbird to do an eagle's work, but He loves both the hummingbirds and the eagles."

"Well, that's a relief to me. I wouldn't have a chance any other way."

They trudged on, and Dai's eyes darted everywhere. Now and then he saw boys and girls lurking behind broken stone walls or peering out of windows. "These children seem so alone, and they're all so pitiful," he told Mei-Lani. "I feel sorry for them."

"There! You see? That's one of the good things about you. You really care about people."

"Well, these little kids, who wouldn't care about them?"

Mei-Lani said sadly, "You'd be surprised at how many people don't care about anyone except themselves. You take Heck, for instance. He hasn't wasted any pity on these children."

Dai hadn't thought about that, but he nodded. "Heck's pretty self-centered, but he's a good fellow."

"He's a conniving, manipulating hustler," Mei-Lani said flatly.

"Don't you like him?"

"Yes, I like him, but I like him for what's underneath and for what he could be. Not for the way he acts most of the time."

They stopped occasionally and went inside buildings. They found homes that were so covered with dust and every sign of decay that each time they were glad to be outside again.

Finally Mei-Lani said, "We may as well start back and report. It doesn't look like we're going to find anything, and it's going to be getting dark soon."

"All right, then." He touched the Neuromag pistol

on his belt and said, "I guess I didn't need to bring this after all."

"No. There doesn't seem to be any danger here. But you wouldn't be afraid even if there were."

Dai felt his face redden. "I don't know whether I would or not. It depends on what we saw." Something had been on his mind, and abruptly he said, "You know, I never have been very good with girls. I guess I've always felt . . . awkward."

"You're the least awkward boy I've ever seen. Why, you can turn back flips just like an acrobat."

Dai laughed, and the sound echoed down the deserted street. "That's what I need to do. Turn back flips to get attention from girls."

"I know which girl you're thinking of," Mei-Lani said calmly and watched his eyes, her lips curving upward in a smile. "You're thinking of Raina."

This time Dai did blush.

"She really likes you, Dai."

"She wouldn't like me."

"There you go again. I'm going to have to get a stick—a big one!"

Dai thought that Mei-Lani, as always, had a way of making things seem better. "All right. I'll look for a big one for you."

They walked rapidly now, for darkness was quickly falling, and it was a murky darkness, somewhat depressing.

Dai began to whistle softly; then he began singing the words to a song that came out of the Scripture:

"As the deer pants for the water
 So my soul longs for you.
 You alone are my heart's desire
 And I long to worship you.

You alone are my strength, my shield.
To you, oh, Lord, may my spirit yield.
You alone are my heart's desire,
And I long to worship you."

"That's a beautiful song, Dai," Mei-Lani said. "Where did you learn it?"

"I learned it from my aunt. She knows lots of hymns like that."

"Sing it again."

Dai obediently began singing, this time louder and more powerfully. He had a sweet and clear voice with a wide range.

Mei-Lani quickly learned the tune and words and began to sing along with him.

And then something caught Dai's eye. He looked to the side and saw children coming out of the houses and alleyways. A small crowd was gathering behind them. He and Mei-Lani continued walking down the street, and the boys and girls followed closely, their numbers increasing all the time.

"Keep on singing, Dai," Mei-Lani whispered. "Keep singing the same song. The children love it."

He glanced back at the crowd behind them and began to sing louder. The sound of the song filled the street and floated on the darkening air.

And then it was that Dai Bando and Mei-Lani Lao received a great shock. Dai was singing. Mei-Lani was singing. And suddenly, at the same time, they both realized that the children were singing with them!

Dai was so stunned that he broke off and gasped, "Listen! Do you hear that?"

"Yes, they're singing the words along with us! They *can* communicate, after all!"

Even as she was saying this, two of the children

ventured up close. Their red skin glowed, and their eyes were filled with love. One took Mei-Lani's arm; the other grasped Dai's. They pulled eagerly at them, and motioned with their free hands.

"They want us to go with them," Dai said. "I can understand that much."

"Then, come on, Dai. Maybe we've stumbled onto something."

9

The Captain Is Shot Down

Raina, Heck, and Ivan Petroski worked on the computer system in the metal building for more than three hours.

It was a most difficult job, for these computers differed from any that they had ever seen. Most computers had input devices such as keyboards, pointers, and trackballs that gave the computer commands. Not these!

Ivan had been standing on Heck's shoulders, trying to get a better look at the top sections of the apparatus. "Heck," he complained. "Will you stand *still?*"

"You may be a dwarf, but you're heavier than me. I don't know how much longer I can hold you!" Heck groused back.

Petroski jumped off Heck's shoulders to the floor, just missing Heck's huge front. "You've got to do something about your weight. Your stomach is becoming dangerous to us all," Ivan admonished as he stood eyeball to belly in front of Heck.

Heck, rubbing his shoulders, shrugged. "I love to eat. There, it's out! Everyone knows now. I LOVE TO EAT!" he yelled at the top of his lungs.

Raina, who had been studying the intricate engravings on the metal surface of the equipment, quickly changed the subject. "These engravings are not just for looks," she said confidently. "I believe that in some way they are inputs to the computers. I've traced all the ones I can reach, though, and nothing happens."

Ivan retorted, "Then how do you know you're right?"

"Call it woman's intuition! Something tells me that whoever designed this machinery just communicated very differently than we do."

While Ivan piled up boxes and chairs to get to the topmost section of the computer, Heck and Raina worked side by side. Heck was using his instruments to check out various systems, all the while explaining to Raina that most computer systems are basically the same.

"I know they seem a lot different, Raina," he said cheerfully, "but they're really about the same. They use languages, you know."

"Then I guess Mei-Lani really ought to be working on this," Raina ventured. "Or Ringo. How did *we* get assigned this job?"

"It's not that kind of language. I'm not good on real languages myself. Someone told me once that real linguists make good musicians, and vice versa. They both require an ear, don't you see? You have to be able to hear things."

"What do you mean by a computer language, then?"

"Computers speak to each other by using impulses, whether these impulses are electrical, chemical, or biological. The impulses are the language of computers. No impulses means the computer does nothing! We just have to find out what kind of impulses this computer uses."

"Heck, have you ever seen *anything* like this machine?"

He smiled. "No, but that's what makes it all the more fascinating for me. And, I hope, *I* will become more fascinating to you."

Heck jabbered on for some time, turning occasionally to glance at Raina.

She rarely looked at him, and she knew this was irritating, for Heck Jordan liked to be admired.

"What I like about computers," he said after a while, "is that you can depend on them."

Raina did turn to smile at him that time. "I'd really rather depend on people."

"Nah, people will let you down, but computers won't."

"Now, Heck, we both know that computers can fail." And then she smiled right into his eyes. "But what you've said makes me think. Machines can fail us, and—you're right—other people can fail us, but God will never fail us."

Heck always acted nervous whenever any of his friends began talking about God. He alone among the ensigns was not a Christian, and he seemed to feel he had to defend himself.

"I don't know if I'd want God on my side. I've read enough of the Bible to know that He put a few people through some pretty rough times," he told her. "Think about old Jonah. Got swallowed up by a whale, and Daniel got thrown in a lions' den."

"Yes, they did," Raina said. "But Daniel got out of the lions' den, because God sent an angel to close the lions' mouths. And God caused the whale to spit Jonah up on dry land. He was watching over them both, even in the whale's belly and the lions' den."

"Well, you can excuse me. I'm staying out of lions' dens and whale's bellies."

"How can you know that for sure, Heck?" Raina asked patiently. "We're in a dangerous profession. Don't you remember when that awful monster nearly got Jerusha? If Ringo hadn't been there, she would have been killed."

"You won't catch me volunteering for anything dangerous."

Raina continued to probe the computer, but she really felt far out of her element. She knew that Heck was the best electronics man on board the *Daystar*. If she hadn't known it, he had told her often enough. Again she felt compassion for Heck. She thought he covered a rather good heart with a lot of bluster and boasting.

After a while Raina said, "Did you ever stop to think why you're so good with electronics, Heck?"

"I'm smart, that's why!"

"Were you born smart, or did you just learn how to be smart?"

"Are you kidding?" The surprise etched across his freckled face was a good indicator that he didn't know where she was going with this. "I was born smart!"

Raina pounced on that. "So you were created intelligent, with all of your abilities, and you really can't take credit for them. But who gave them to you?"

Heck began to squirm.

He knows the answer well enough, Raina thought. *He just hates to give in.*

"I don't know," he muttered.

"Yes, you do," she said firmly. "*God* gave you a genius for electronics, and you need to thank Him for your gifts instead of just using them for your own personal gain."

"Wait a minute, now!" Heck whirled around and pointed at her with the small screwdriver he held in his hand. "What you're saying doesn't make any sense, Raina."

"Of course, it does. Suppose you had some money and . . ."

"I wish I did! Someday I'm going to."

"Well, let's just suppose that you do, and suppose you gave it to an investment counselor back on Earth. Then suppose you came back in a year and asked for the interest your money had earned. And *then* suppose that the investment counselor said, 'Oh, I didn't invest it. I just kept it in a safe.'"

"I'd get me a new investment counselor, that's what!"

Raina moved closer to Heck. "But don't you see, that's what you're doing to God. He gave you certain abilities. He gives everyone abilities. Not all of them are spectacular. Some of them seem very minor, but whatever He gives us, we are to use it for His glory."

"I don't understand all this, Raina, and I'm not interested. I just want to get rich and have everything money can buy."

Raina felt a sadness in her heart. She had not been joking about the dangers of their profession, and she well knew that each voyage they made might be the last for all of them. She tried once more, saying gently, "Heck, God loves you and is waiting for you to change your mind."

Heck was clearly flustered. He dropped his screwdriver, picked it up, wagged his head at her. "Don't be preaching at me, Raina. I've heard enough preaching for a lifetime."

At that moment Ivan let out a yelp. The boxes that he was standing on suddenly rocked back and forth, and he fell over with a crash.

"Ivan, are you all right?" Raina rushed to the chief engineer and grabbed his hand. "Can I help you up?"

"Take your grubby hands off me!" Ivan yelled. "I don't need help!" He was small but made up for his lack of height with a quick temper. He scrambled to his feet by himself, and his dark brown eyes were snapping. "Well, now that you amateurs have failed, it's time for an expert to find all the answers. Namely, me."

Heck began straightening up boxes. "What are you talking about? What answers?"

"About this computer. I knew you geniuses weren't any good. It takes an all-around man like me to get to the bottom of things."

"What did you find out, Ivan?" Raina asked. "I'm sure it's wonderful."

"I found out how this computer talks."

Heck seized Petroski by the arm. "What do you mean? You discovered the kind of language it uses?"

"What else could I mean? Turn loose of me!" Ivan waited until Heck removed his hands, and then he gloated. "Ever since we made a nursery out of this ship with you babies on board, I knew it wasn't going to work."

"Oh, Ivan, don't tease us! What did you find out?" Raina cried.

"That this computer doesn't speak in regular binary bit."

"What does it use, then?" Heck asked, wide-eyed.

"It uses tonal melodies to communicate."

Heck and Raina stared at each other blankly, then turned their eyes back to the screen.

"Does it really, Ivan?" Raina said. "How clever of you to discover it!"

"Yes, it was clever, wasn't it? Well, let's find out if we can interpret some of these melodies."

Raina placed herself beside Ivan, and the two began working. Heck wandered over to the large, central apparatus and began to examine it more closely. Stroking its sides, he murmured, "That's all right, baby.

I'm going to get to the bottom of you yet. You just wait and see."

Night had fallen by the time Captain Edge got back to the *Daystar*. The sky was full of stars, and, as always, he glanced upward toward the Great Orion Nebula. It looked like a gigantic green dove alighting on the ground. He started thinking, *What a sight! I can't think of anything I'd rather be doing than be in the middle of all of this. Orion is such a beautiful constellation!*

Greeted by the sentry on guard, he entered the ship and went directly to the sick bay. He did not really expect to find Temple Cole there, but he knew that sometimes she worked late. Since she wasn't in her work area, he continued on down the corridor to the cruiser's living quarters. He touched the button on Dr. Cole's door, and almost at once it opened before him.

Temple got up from a couch where evidently she had been reading a book. She was wearing a silk gown that was a soft, violet color that matched her eyes.

"I didn't expect you to be back so early, Captain."

"I just got in. I went to the sick bay, but you weren't there. Have you got a minute?"

"Of course. Come in. Let me order you something to eat."

"No, I'll stop by the galley later and get a sandwich."

"Well, something to drink then. Coffee, perhaps."

"That would be good." He threw himself down into one of the leather, contoured chairs and watched as she crossed the cabin to brew the coffee. When she brought a cup back to him, he took it and sipped gratefully. "Thanks. That's good. I forgot to eat today."

"What did you find out, Captain?"

101

"'Captain'? Have we gotten back to that? I thought it was Temple and Mark."

Temple Cole flushed, as though she had deliberately chosen to use his title rather than his name. She wanted no romantic entanglements with her commanding officer, she'd told him—though on the *Daystar*'s first mission, she had seemed very attracted to him. Now she said simply, "I suppose first names are all right as long as we're alone. Otherwise, we'd better use our titles."

Mark Edge was not quite satisfied with that but could find no way to argue against it. "Tell me about the children," he said.

Temple spoke rapidly, telling him of the tests she had run. She ended her report by saying, "They're all very young. None over fifteen or sixteen, I would say—although, of course, we didn't test them all. Some could be just a little bit older."

"Did you find out anything else?"

The doctor nodded and leaned toward him, excitement in her eyes. "I found out one other thing. Dai brought some clothes back. You know—some of those that you found abandoned."

"Yes, I told him to. I thought they might offer something. What about them?"

"It's the strangest thing, Mark. The clothes are all made out of synthetic materials."

Edge lifted an eyebrow. "What's odd about that?"

"The clothes contain no DNA. No human trace elements."

"I'm afraid I don't get it."

"Our skin and hair shed all the time. So any garment we wear picks up DNA and trace elements. In this case, it's as if—well, it's as if the clothes had never been used. But they *have* been used, because some of them are worn. You can tell—especially from the shoes. Some of the sides are run over; some of them have very worn heels. The clothes don't *look* new, either. You can just tell."

Mark Edge frowned and sipped absently at his coffee. "What do you make of that?"

A puzzled look came into Temple Cole's violet eyes. "I've thought a lot about it, and all I can come up with is that somehow all of the adult humans, all their DNA, and all their trace elements were pulled right out of their synthetic clothes."

"Does that help us? I don't see it."

"I don't understand it, either. But everything about this is a mystery." She sat back, as though setting the topic aside. "Tell me about the city. I'd like to go there tomorrow."

"I'll take you." Captain Edge launched into a description of all that he had seen in Tyrian, while she listened attentively. Finally he rose, put his cup down, and got ready to leave.

When she got up, he leaned over to kiss her.

At once Temple put her hand on his chest and stepped backwards, freeing herself.

"What's this? Why are you so standoffish, Temple? I've kissed you good night before this."

Temple shook her head firmly. She must have had it all thought out, for she said, "If we ever kiss again, Mark, it will be for the right reasons. For now, I'm a member of your crew. You are my superior officer, and that's all there is to it."

Offended, Mark Edge stared at her, then spun around and left without another word.

10

A Language in Song

Dai and Mei-Lani allowed the Tyrian children to lead them by the hand back into the huge metal building. Dai sensed that the boys and girls all seemed far happier than had been their custom. Their eyes were bright, and many of them crowded around their visitors, trying to touch one or the other, as if for reassurance.

"Something's happened to change them. But I don't know what," Dai murmured, marveling.

"Whatever it is, it's wonderful. It's made them very happy."

"It seems to have something to do with the singing."

"I think so too, though I can't imagine what." Mei-Lani wagged her head sadly, saying, "It's such a handicap not being able to communicate with them."

Dai gave her a quick smile. She was a very sensitive and sympathetic young lady, he thought, and right now she seemed even younger than she actually was. "Well, we'll just have to trust the Lord," he said, "to give us some way to communicate."

"I have been praying about that," Mei-Lani said. "We have no answer yet, but the Lord doesn't always answer the first time we ask, does He? Or in the way we expect."

Dai Bando grinned. "And it's a good thing. Some of the things I've asked for, I really didn't need at all. I probably would have hurt myself if I had gotten them."

With boys and girls still trailing behind, they walked through the large conference area to the adjoining room, where they found Raina and Ivan busily working at the computer.

Ivan glared at them and glared at the children. *"What's going on here?"* he growled.

"We haven't been able to talk with any of these kids," Dai announced, "but we found out they can *sing!"*

Ivan's attention immediately focused on Dai, and then he looked past him at the boys and girls. "What do you mean, 'sing'? I haven't heard them say a word."

Mei-Lani explained excitedly. "When Dai started singing out in the street, boys and girls just came out of everywhere. The singing seemed to draw them, and after a while they started singing along with us!"

"Is that right? Hm. Well, then. That goes right along with what I found out here. Didn't I tell you, Raina?"

"Ivan's found out that the computer works on *tonal* messages, and I believe we can use our linguistic comcorder to communicate with them." Raina pointed to the communications device that she always carried on her belt. "All languages have similarities. Humans have to do the same sort of things no matter what planet they're on. This instrument simply identifies a language group, translates it, and then repeats it in our language. All we need is to record some of the tonal melodies the children use."

When Raina had explained the device to Dai and Mei-Lani, she said, "Could you get them to sing some more?"

"I guess we can try." Dai shrugged. "They seem to like it." He began to sing the familiar hymn, and at once all the children joined in with him.

"At least now we know they've got vocal cords," Ivan growled. "Dai, look at that chair over there and point at it, and sing the word *chair.*"

Dai looked at the diminutive engineer as if he had lost his mind. "Point at the chair and sing the word *chair?* That's what you want me to do?"

"That's right! Just do what I tell you!" Ivan barked.

"All engineers are strange," Dai muttered under his breath. However, he pointed and sang as clearly as he could the word *chair.*

At once many of the children sang back a single syllable. Some of them had high voices, some lower. They almost harmonized.

"See," Ivan said, "that's their word for *chair,* but it has to be sung. Now go around and point at other things. Mei-Lani, this is your area. You work with them and try to figure it all out."

"All right, I'll try. Raina, I don't understand that comcorder, so you come along and tell me what to do."

"We have to get down enough of their basic language," Raina said as they started off, "so we can form a grammar. If we have vocabulary and grammar, then we can make up sentences."

The next hour was exciting to all of them. Dai watched Mei-Lani and Raina take turns pointing to objects, including themselves. Each time they did, the children, who had caught on at once, would sing out their interpretations in their tonal language.

At last Mei-Lani said, her eyes glowing with satisfaction, "Dai, I think we have enough to communicate some with them now. At least I know enough to start."

Dai felt like singing for joy. He began the song that the boys and girls had first heard, "As the Deer Pants." He sang very softly.

The children gathered around him, all joining in.

They sang the song with him all the way through. Oddly, they occasionally pointed toward the big, mysterious device with the swirling red lights.

"They seem to be trying to tell us something about that thing, whatever it is," Mei-Lani said.

Ivan looked thoughtful. "As soon as we're able to talk to them on a higher level, surely one of them ought to be able to tell us what it is."

Ivan was a feisty individual who loved challenges, and now he said in a demanding voice, "Well, everybody get busy! That's what we're here for! The captain didn't send us here to take a vacation!" He turned his back on everyone else and began tinkering with a computer.

The *Daystar* Space Rangers went back to trying to communicate with the children.

Captain Edge glanced at the figures that Bronwen Llewellen had put before him. He knew she was an expert navigator, perhaps the best in the entire Intergalactic Fleet, but he hated to admit that the numbers she'd jotted down and the charts she had drawn were entirely over his head. Nevertheless, he knew that there was no bluffing with this silver-haired woman. He said humbly, "So what does all this mean?"

"I think it means, Captain," Zeno Thrax cut in, "that the red comet is going to miss this planet but not by much."

"It will be very close," Bronwen agreed. She looked tired, for she had labored for hours over the charts and figures. Now she gnawed at her lower lip nervously. "The *Daystar* computer systems now are at only thirty-five percent efficiency. That's not good. We're just limping along."

"Yes, Captain," Thrax agreed, "and when that

comet comes by and brushes against us, more or less, our computers won't be any good at all. We'll be dead in the water."

Impatiently, Edge asked, "Do we know why?"

Thrax looked up at the captain with his colorless eyes. "The tail of the red comet consists of billions of ionized hydrogen atoms. As the comet gets closer, it will travel through the Great Orion Nebula. The nebula is also composed of ionized hydrogen atoms."

Edge scratched his head. "I still don't see the problem . . ."

Thrax replied. "The problem is with the nebula. It also contains nebulium lines of gases that have been identified with lines of doubly ionized oxygen."

"So that's it." Edge continued the first officer's thought. "What you're saying is that when the comet races through the nebula, the ionized gases will collide, producing an electromagnetic pulse fifty light-years in diameter. No wonder we have problems."

"I think, since the comet is only hours away, it might be best to shut down most of the computer system," Zeno suggested.

"And what about the crew that's in the city?"

"We'd better bring them back to the *Daystar* right away. The ship has the best protection against radiation, wouldn't you think?"

"The *Daystar* and that metal building," Edge said. "We'll have to get the children into that." He was lost in thought for a while, then said, "All right. We'll bring them back right now. Number One, see to it."

"Aye, Captain. I'll call them back at once."

Ringo was playing checkers with Studs Cagney. The burly crew chief prided himself on his playing ability and had won the *Daystar* checkers tournament just the week before. Now he grinned, jumped three of Ringo's men, and then slammed his fist on the board. "Gotcha!" he exclaimed. "That makes three out of three."

Ringo ran both hands through his hair in a gesture of futility. "I don't see how you do that. I've always been good at games like this as well as at computers. I've learned how to think ahead on all these moves, and still you beat me."

"That's the reason I beat you."

"Why?" Ringo said. "Because I know computers?"

"Nope." Studs grinned. He leaned back and took a drink of the dark liquid in the heavy tumbler beside him. "Ah, that's good cider," he said. He was a rough man and had been a rather brutal one. Since encountering Dai Bando, though, Studs Cagney had become surprisingly more gentle. "You *think*. That's the reason I beat you."

"Checkers *is* a thinking game!" Ringo protested.

"No, it ain't. I don't ever think. I just play."

"You don't ever try to plan ahead?"

"Never. I don't do none of that stuff. I just play the game. You know what they said about the long-ago Marines—don't plan, just improvise."

The very thought frustrated Ringo, for he had a scientific mind. But he knew that Studs, somehow, had the ability to play checkers without a mathematical mind. He said, "I sure don't understand it. But you know, Studs, it's strange. There have been people all through history that could do remarkable things that couldn't be explained."

"Like what?"

"Well, Mei-Lani was telling me that there was a blind black man who lived during the American Civil War. He was almost unable to learn anything, but someone sat him down at a piano and five minutes later he was playing it."

"He never took no lessons?"

"Never had a lesson in his life," Ringo said. There was wonder in his voice. "He could hear any tune, no matter how long, and play it on the piano. Never made a mistake."

"I ain't never heard of nothin' like that."

"He never knew how he did it, of course. They tried to fool him," Ringo said. "Mei-Lani told me that they'd bring in concert pianists and have them play pieces that lasted thirty minutes, and sometimes they'd put a mistake in. Well, blind Tom would just play them over with all the mistakes included. No one ever could figure out how he did it."

"Well, that's the way I play checkers. I don't know how I do it. I just do it."

Ringo got up and began to pace around nervously. "I wish they'd come back from that city. I don't feel right about all this."

"Well, I don't feel any too good about it myself," Studs said. Absentmindedly he pushed checkers around on the board. "They say that comet's coming right at us. If it hits, we're *kaboom!*"

"That's what I hear, too." Ringo hesitated, then said, "If it does hit us, we'll all be killed."

"That's right." Studs grinned back toughly. "But if it does kill us, it won't kill us but once."

Ringo gazed at the muscular crew chief. "Are you afraid of dying, Studs?"

"Naw, I don't think about it. Just like playing checkers—I just live and don't worry about it."

"I don't think dying's quite the same thing as checkers," Ringo said thoughtfully. He himself was only a new Christian, but he felt the need to express his faith, such as it was, to the crew chief.

"I'm not much of a Christian," he went on. "Not like Raina or Bronwen Llewellen, but I don't think it's a good idea to leave such an important thing to chance."

"Yeah, I know. Dai Bando's been talking to me about that. He's about got me convinced that there's something to it."

"You're still not a Christian, though?"

"Nope, but I'm thinkin' about it." Studs got up and went to look out the porthole. He seemed to be scanning the skies for the red comet that could snuff out his life. For a long time he said nothing, but then he came back, murmuring, "Maybe I ought to listen a little bit closer to what Dai's been telling me. And you too."

Ringo wished he had more confidence, but he himself was still a rather confused young man. He was disturbed because he did not know who his parents were. Reaching into his shirt, he pulled out the medallion and stared at it, noticing again the motto that he couldn't interpret.

"What's that?" Studs asked

"This was the only thing that was with me when they found me outside the door at the orphanage."

Studs moved closer. "Is that right? You grew up in an orphanage, eh?"

"That's right. I did."

"I hope it wasn't as bad as my raisin' was." He leaned closer and said, "Who's that fellow on the medal?"

"I don't know. I'd like to find out. Maybe someday I'll meet up with someone who can read this writing."

"It ain't proper writin'," Studs observed.

"No, it's some sort of foreign language, but not

even Mei-Lani has seen anything like it. I'd like to find out, though. It's kind of bad not knowing who your dad was."

Studs muttered, "I knew who mine was. All I ever got from him was the back of his hand and a cussing out." He went back to the porthole. "Well, it's comin'. We'll know pretty soon if we're gonna make it or not."

Ringo left the rec room and went to the larger porthole on the bridge. He could see the stars sparkling out in the dark night, and somewhere among them a red comet was approaching at tremendous speed.

Ringo suddenly found himself praying. "Oh, God, don't let me die before I've found out about myself." On second thought, that seemed a rather selfish prayer. He tried to explain himself better by saying, "It's not just me, but I wouldn't want to see Heck die. He's not ready, and you know how I feel about Raina, even if she doesn't know it. And the crew, I don't want any of them to die, so I'm asking You to take care of us."

He paused, still dissatisfied with the prayer, but he could not think of a way to say it any better. He walked away from the skyport, his shoulders stooped as he thought of the red comet rushing toward them.

11

The Mystery Solved

The conference room on board the *Daystar* was barely large enough to hold all of those who had gathered there. Edge, Petroski, and Thrax were at one end of the table. Temple Cole sat farther down with Bronwen Llewellen beside her. The Space Rangers completed the group.

Raina leaned toward Ringo and whispered, "What's this meeting about?"

"I don't know, Raina. I got the word the same as you—an emergency meeting of all the officers and ensigns. The captain looks excited, though."

Indeed, Capt. Mark Edge did look pleased about something, Raina thought. He also looked nice. He wore a fresh uniform, had just shaved, and there was a liveliness in his bearing that she had missed seeing for the past few days.

She could hear Jerusha and Dr. Cole's quiet comments back and forth.

"The captain's different today," Jerusha said.

"Yes, he seems to be." Dr. Cole nodded slowly. "Do you know what he's so excited about?"

"I suspect it's something that he found out in that computer room in the city."

"From what I hear, he'd better find out something fast," Temple murmured. "That red comet is coming faster than I like. It makes me feel uncomfortable."

Captain Edge stood up then and said cheerfully, "I know you're wondering why I've called you all together. Well, I have good news. We have finally been able—in spite of interference from the red comet—to get some information from the computer system inside the city." With a smile he glanced at Ensign Heck Jordan and Chief Petroski. "And for that we have to give most of the credit to Heck and Ivan. We owe them a debt of thanks."

Petroski waved his hand airily and said, "I knew I could do it."

Heck glared at him and scowled. "*We* did it, Chief!"

"Oh! Well, I always can use a helper," Petroski said graciously.

The captain interrupted. "There's credit enough to go around. But, basically, what has happened is that Heck was able to interface our linguistic comcorder to that computer's hardware. As a result, we've been able to pull files out of the computer system so that now we can be pretty sure what this mystery's all about."

"And this planet *is* certainly a mystery, sir," Zeno Thrax said. "I've never seen anything like it in my life."

"I doubt that any of us ever has, First. But I think now we've got it. What we get from the Tyrian computer is that it seems this planet was once inhabited by normal colonists from Earth. Well, 'normal' to us except for their color. They had a scarlet tinge to their skin.

"Tyrian's water supply has been diminishing for quite some time. In those early days, as now, pumps brought drinking water to the planet's surface. Now, what we've found out is that their skin color and their lack of normal physical growth were both caused by an exotic form of the cochineal virus. This virus existed in the lowest regions of the water table. It was also so small that the usual filter system failed to keep it from the drinking supply."

116

"That would explain it, then!" Temple Cole exclaimed excitedly. "Why didn't I think of that?"

"What does it mean?" Jerusha frowned. "I don't understand any of this."

"As I understand it," Captain Edge said, "the cochineal virus uses its DNA to reprogram human cells. No other negative effects have been noticed. On the other hand, it delayed aging. It kept everyone young! That part's good, but few people would want to come and live here because of the virus. Besides, this planet is little more than a dried-out rock."

Raina felt bewildered. "I still don't really understand this, sir," she said. "Could you be a little bit more specific?"

"As best as I can get it—and we haven't found out all we need to know yet—the virus doesn't affect other parts of the global environment. What it does do is make people live an awfully long time. No one has died of old age since the planet was first colonized three hundred years ago!"

"Wow!" Heck said. "Maybe we could bottle this virus and take it back to Earth and sell it all through the galaxy." His eyes glowed, and Raina could see he was exploring the possibilities. "Why, we could make a fortune! People on Earth are doing everything they can to live longer—all kinds of diets and exercise and pills —and here we've got the answer. We're all going to be rich!"

"I doubt if that would be approved by the Intergalactic Council, and it certainly wouldn't be wise," Bronwen Llewellen told him. She leaned forward in her chair and fixed her dark blue eyes on Heck. "Long life isn't the answer to happiness. Sometimes it just means more misery."

"That's true," Mei-Lani said. "Didn't you ever read *Gulliver's Travels*, Heck?"

"Who was Gulliver?" he asked in response.

"He was a character in a book written a long, long time ago. He found some people that had learned how to live forever, but they were miserable."

"Why would they be miserable?" Heck looked truly puzzled.

"Because though they had long life, they had all of the problems of old age. So Gulliver decided he didn't want to be like them, and I wouldn't either."

"No, God has given man a certain length of time to live," Bronwen said quietly. "After that, He wants us to go to be with Him. Then, in that place, we'll all have new bodies that will indeed be forever young. But that's *heaven*, Heck, and you can't buy that or bottle it or peddle it as you do cough medicine."

Heck slumped back in his chair and muttered, "Every time I think of a scheme to get rich and famous, you people shoot it down in flames."

"Well, we'll leave Heck pondering ways to get rich," Captain Edge said with a wry smile. "But here's the important thing. Tyrian began to run out of water. So, many years ago, they started building a colony ship."

Edge glanced at Heck. The ensign was clearly fuming mad at being talked down to. Then the huge German shepherd, her black tail wagging, padded over and sat beside his chair, as though trying to console him.

Glad that Heck had taken Contessa's attention away from him, Edge continued his explanation. "They decided to build the craft to resemble an oversized hotel, so they constructed it in a mall in the center of the city. They stocked the ship with all the supplies

118

they would need for a long journey. And then all the families in the area prepared to move into it. That was just two years ago."

"Where were they going?" Zeno Thrax asked. "And why didn't they go?"

"They were headed for the planet Deton, thousands of light-years away. In order to make the voyage, their plan—according to the information we got—was to transform the colony population into energy patterns."

"To do *what?*" Dai Bando exclaimed. "Turn people into energy? Is that possible? And why would they want to do that?"

"For one thing, it's a lot easier to store energy patterns," Edge said with a grimace, "than it is to transport people."

"I wouldn't want to be turned into a blip of energy," Jerusha said.

"Neither would I," Edge said, "but that's what they tried to do. In preparation for space travel, the adults began storing their energy patterns in a big device within the structure. The red sparkles of light that we saw are actually those energy patterns! Then, unexpectedly, the red comet headed this way. It knocked out their computers."

"Wait! Wait a minute!" Temple Cole exclaimed. "Then that's why you found clothes everywhere!"

"That's right. Each adult had been turned into energy patterns. They had a system in place to care for the children too. But, unfortunately, at that point the comet erased the instructions in the computer before that step was taken. The equipment hasn't worked since then—until now." Edge ran a hand across his jaw. "So the children were left."

"And they've had to fend for themselves these last

two years," Bronwen whispered. "Is that right, Captain?"

"I believe that's right, Navigator. They've had to fend for themselves without much knowledge and only the older children to take care of them. They've been eating the ship's supplies all this time. I'm afraid not all of them have lived."

"I think we came just in time, Captain," Jerusha said quietly. "I think God must have sent us here. They look strange to us with their red color, but that doesn't matter to God. He's interested in all His creation."

"I can see that," Captain Edge agreed. "But the question is, what happens next?"

"We're helpless, Captain," Bronwen said. "Our computers won't work. The ship is dead for all practical purposes. All we can do is hide in here and wait until the comet passes. Then, God willing, we can do something."

12

The Crimson Sky

Mei-Lani was playing checkers with Studs Cagney, and to his disgust she had beaten him two games in a row.

"I ain't never been beat playin' checkers!" he snorted in disgust. "And now to get beat by a girl! Why, it's enough to make a fellow half sick!"

"Why is it worse being beaten by a girl than by a boy?" Mei-Lani asked with a smile.

"I don't know," Studs said, staring in disbelief at the checkerboard. "It just is." He frowned at her suspiciously, then asked, "Where'd you learn to play checkers?"

"You taught me!"

"You never played before then?"

"No, not that I can remember."

Studs threw up his hands. "Well, that just beats everything. Ain't this a pretty come off? Now I've lost my championship!"

"No, Studs, we were just playing for fun," Mei-Lani said quickly. She saw that his pride had been wounded, and now she wished that she had arranged to lose the last game. "Let's play just one more," she suggested.

Studs glared. "What you got on that mind of yours?"

"Nothing, Studs. I just thought we'd play another game. We don't have anything else to do but wait."

"Yeah, that's right. Wait." Studs glanced nervously at the porthole. "That ball of fire's on its way, and here we sit playing checkers. All right, this time I'll take the blacks. Maybe it'll bring me better luck."

Mei-Lani actually had not played checkers before Studs introduced her to the game, but she seemed to have a natural flair for it. However, this time she saw to it that she lost after a hard-fought game. More than once she saw jumps that she chose to ignore, for she did not want to hurt Cagney's feelings.

"Now," Studs said, after his victory. "This is something more like it." His eyes gleamed, and he rubbed his hands together with pleasure. "Let's make it the best four out of five."

"I really can't, Studs. Not now. I have some work to do. I've been working on the language of the crimson children. I need to record some information."

"Funny little tykes, ain't they?" Studs murmured. Then he shifted nervously and said, "You know what? I think we got to do something to help 'em."

"Captain Edge and Ivan have scanned the ship. Ivan says that everything is all right in engineering. The ship is functional."

"Well, maybe the machinery's all right, but what's gonna happen to them kids when that comet sashays by?"

"The captain wants them all in their spacecraft in order to have protection from radiation," Mei-Lani said slowly. "Some of them are no more than four or five years old."

"Well, that tears it! Come on! Let's go!"

"Where are we going?"

"Don't be like a woman, always asking questions! Just do what I tell you!"

Mei-Lani grinned at the crusty crew chief. "All right, Studs."

She followed as he barreled his way past other

members of the crew. He had a way of walking as if he expected people to simply step aside, and most of them had learned to. Several of them had been bowled over by his cannonball type of explosive walking.

When he reached the engine room, he found Dai Bando cleaning the Mark V engine control panel. "Come on, Dai. We're volunteering."

"What's up, Studs?"

"That comet's coming, and the captain wants all those kids inside that big building. Make sure they're all under shelter. We're going to do it."

"That sounds good to me. I'm with you." Dai put his hand on the crew chief's muscular shoulder and smiled warmly. "It was kind of you to think of them, Studs."

Mei-Lani thought the compliment embarrassed Studs, and he made a face. "Don't be makin' a saint out of me!"

"I'm expecting you'll reach sainthood one day," Mei-Lani said. "And it *was* kind of you."

"Well, you can pin a medal on me later." But Cagney grinned. "Now, let's go do what we can for those poor kids."

They found Captain Edge and told him they were volunteering to get the children into safety.

The captain looked relieved. "Great," he said. "I was just about to designate a crew to do that."

Mei-Lani, Dai, and Studs quickly walked to the city. It was not hard to gather the boys and girls together. All Dai had to do was raise his voice in song outside the spaceship structure, and the street was suddenly swarming with ragged, happy children. For some reason, their red skins did not seem so unusual anymore.

Mei-Lani sang to them, "Come on inside. I'll teach you a new song."

"We'll go round up all the strays, Mei-Lani," Studs said. "If we get them all together here, maybe they'll be protected when that comet goes by."

Raina closed her eyes and leaned back. She rubbed them wearily and blinked. "I wish I were smarter."

Heck would never admit that he was not smart enough to do anything. Nevertheless, his frustration showed as he poked at the keyboard harder than was absolutely necessary. "I'll find it," he said. "Don't worry, Raina, I'll find it."

Raina watched the boy doggedly key away. "You haven't slept since we've gotten here, Heck. You must be exhausted."

"I'm all right. Don't bother me."

"Sometimes there are problems human beings just can't solve. It won't do any good to make yourself sick."

"Who says I can't solve this?" Heck said pugnaciously. He did draw back from the computer long enough to reach into a sack of sweets. He removed the yellow wrapper from a piece of candy, popped it into his mouth, considered the sack, then did the same with four more pieces. Then he immediately went back to glowering at the screen and mumbling around the bits of hard candy in his mouth.

"You're going to kill yourself eating all that candy."

"Be a pleasant way to die," Heck muttered. His voice was muffled by the candy. "Everybody's got to die some way. I never heard of anybody dying from overeating candy."

"Yes, you have, too. You know that people who don't eat right don't usually live as long as people who do."

"I don't believe in all that stuff. I don't even believe in vitamins."

"What do you mean, you don't believe in vitamins?"

"Did you ever see one?" Heck said. "I mean, did you ever see one single vitamin, Raina?"

"Of course not. Nobody has."

"Then how do you know they're there?"

Raina was accustomed to Heck's outlandish statements, so she merely smiled at him, knowing that he was only trying to provoke an argument. "You're just mad because you can't reverse the energy patterns and turn the inhabitants back into their human form. Aren't you? Aren't you, Heck?"

"I'm gonna find it. Just hang on! Don't rush me!"

"I'm not rushing you," Raina said. She went back to work for a while on her own computer.

The two of them had been at this for long hours, and every time Raina had made a suggestion, Heck stubbornly ignored it. "It's all in the hardware," he kept saying. "No sense fooling with anything else."

"I'm not so sure." Raina smoothed her auburn hair back over her head and worked on.

She felt as strongly as Heck Jordan did about trying to recover the lost colonists. She thought back over her life, which had not been particularly happy. She had never recovered from the loss of her parents. Their house had burned down, and her father had died saving her. Later, her mother had died from her burns. Since then, Raina had been very much alone. She had this in common with Ringo Smith. Both of them had grown up without the warmth and security of a good family. Ringo had been placed in an orphanage. Raina lived with relatives who were kind, but it was not the same as having her parents.

She had entered the Intergalactic Academy hoping to make some contribution to her world, and then she had been expelled for her Christian beliefs. Now, as she worked alongside Heck, she was praying, *God, please show us how to do this. Show us how to bring back these people. Nothing is too difficult for You.*

"Well, Temple, there it comes!" Edge studied the sky. "And it looks like it'll be a stem-winder."

Dr. Cole, who had accompanied the captain into the city, stopped beside him and looked up, too. "I don't like this, Mark." She was visibly frightened.

So far, the comet was only a mildly reddish spot, but Edge knew things would get worse. "None of us like it. Not much we can do about it, though."

Suddenly he felt a trembling in the earth, very faint, so faint that it was hardly discernible.

Temple grabbed his arm.

He suspected it was an automatic gesture. She was probably not even aware of it, so engrossed was she in what was happening in the canopy of space above the planet.

Edge, however, was very much aware of her touch. Though he knew she was likely not even thinking of him, somehow the touch of her hand through the fabric of his uniform sleeve pleased him.

They both stood looking upward, and the captain said, "We're going to have to ride this one out, Temple."

"Do you think we can?"

"We'll have to. What else can we do?"

Temple Cole sighed. "I must admit that I envy the Rangers. They have such strong Christian faith. As I look out there and know that it won't be long until we'll be right in the middle of what's coming—or at least on the dangerous edge of it—then I realize we may not live through it."

"Always that chance."

Looking at him quickly, she asked, "Doesn't it bother you at all, Mark, that we may be dead soon?"

"Sure, it bothers me!" He was surprised that she should ask. "But one of the first things I learned as a soldier was that you can't go around giving way to your fears."

"But you must feel *something!*"

"You think it would be any better if I talked with a tremor in my voice?"

His light answer made her smile, despite the peril that threatened. "I don't suppose so, but it's good to know that you're a little afraid, too. I always get nervous when I'm around people who are too perfect."

Edge laughed aloud. "You don't have to worry about that. No one ever accused me of being too perfect or even a little perfect. It's just the other way around. Some people make their kids mind by saying, 'Look out, Captain Edge is coming!' They make me out to be a guy with a beard like wire and a voice that grates like pieces of metal rubbing together."

"What's the other side of the picture, Mark?"

"Isn't any."

"Just as well you think so, then." Then she sobered. "I—I'm glad you're here, Mark. I feel safer with you."

"Not much I can do about *that* thing, though," he murmured, motioning toward the reddening sky.

The heavens were, indeed, growing much redder now. There was something sinister about the crimson glow that was beginning to tinge the entire sky over the planet Ciephus.

"I know that. But, Mark, I do know one verse from the Christian Bible."

"What's that?"

"It says somewhere that two are better than one, for if one is alone and falls, who shall lift him up?"

He nodded. "I believe that myself. I've been alone most of my life."

"So have I. Not any fun, is it?"

"Not a lick of fun."

The two continued looking upward. The planet trembled from time to time, almost as if it had been pierced with a sharp instrument and was writhing in pain. The sky grew redder still. And suddenly they were holding hands like children.

Mark Edge was praying—something that he had not really done in a long time.

As the huge red nucleus flew toward Ciephus, the electronic blast wave from the Great Orion Nebula preceded it. Nothing could shield the planet from its computer-damaging electromagnetic pulse.

The giant red comet missed Ciephus by only a quarter of a million miles—a near miss in galactic terms. When the comet flew by, its long feathery tail of red ionized hydrogen bathed the planet in a vibrant red glow.

The tail's particles collided with the Ciephus atmosphere, but the protective ozone layer acted as a global shield. Bronwen estimated that more than 90 percent of the ionized hydrogen never reached the planet's surface. The fiery red display that looked so dangerous turned out to be harmless. But if the computers had been left on, they would have been severely damaged.

Soon the awesome gravitational field of the first magnitude star Betelgeuse once again attracted the rogue comet's flight path. Betelgeuse was more than two hundred sixty million miles in diameter—more than three hundred times larger than the star Sol, in the Earth system.

"Thank You, God, if You're up there somewhere. Thank You for sparing us," Edge said aloud. Then it appeared he noticed everyone's surprised expression and became embarrassed. His stern tone returned. "Bronwen, you and Thrax get our systems back up." He walked off in a huff.

Bronwen turned to Thrax. "I see that the old saying is true."

Thrax finished tying his boot laces before asking, "And what saying is that, madam Navigator?"

"'There are no atheists in foxholes.'"

Thrax looked puzzled. "First, what is a fox? And second, why would someone who does not believe in God want to be in a fox's hole in the first place?"

Bronwen laughed and took Thrax by the arm. "We've got work to do. I'll explain later!"

13

Heck Jordan on Stage

Mei-Lani was standing in the midst of a group of Tyrian children when she looked worriedly across the conference room at Heck Jordan. "What's happening over there, Heck? Are you doing any good?"

"I . . . I think so."

"Good man," Dai said. "I'd sure like to see you make it on this one."

Jerusha was at Heck's right, along with Ivan Petroski. The others were back at the *Daystar*, waiting in the safety of the shield, but these five had stayed in the city for the sake of the children.

Ivan Petroski had denied this, of course.

"I'm *not* stayin' for these kids," he growled. "I'm stayin' because I want to see this problem solved. That's what an engineer does. He solves problems."

Smiling, Jerusha shook her head at that. "I think there's more to it than that, Chief. I think that under that tough outside you've got a real big heart."

Now, Heck had been trying for more than an hour to make the giant computer obey his commands. He declared he had the technical side solved, but still it simply would not respond, and he appeared to be totally frustrated. "I just can't make this blasted thing *work!*" he finally admitted.

His friends stared at him in silence. This was surely the first time Hector Jordan had ever publicly admitted there was something he couldn't do. He actually looked rather pitiful as he stood there.

Jerusha found herself thinking, *He's been sneaky and selfish most of his life, but today something bigger than Heck Jordan is filling his world.*

She suddenly had another thought, though, and she spoke it at once. "I think I know what's wrong, Heck!"

"You're telling me you know more about computers than I do?" Now Heck was angry. "You're an engineer! I'm the electronics expert around here!"

"Yes, you are, and a good one, but I think there's one element that you've left out of all your calculations, Heck," Jerusha said.

"So what's that?"

"A computer would be very much like the people who built it, and you know how these people on Ciephus communicate."

Heck stared at her blankly. "What are you trying to say, Jerusha?"

"Their language is in *song*. Doesn't that tell us something?"

Heck still stared. Then his face flushed. "You're not telling me I've got to *sing* the commands?"

"But I wonder if that wouldn't work. Why don't you try it?"

"I can't sing!"

"I think you're going to have to if you want to be successful," Mei-Lani put in. "It does make sense, Heck. Their whole language is built on tonal melodies. They wouldn't—couldn't—leave that out of their computer programming."

"Go on, Heck. Just try it," Dai urged.

He was even echoed by Chief Petroski, who said, "Go on, smart guy! Let's see you earn your keep! A good electronics man does whatever he has to do to make the equipment work."

132

Heck looked embarrassed, astonished, and a little afraid all at the same time. He glanced over at Raina, and she smiled encouragingly. "Come on, Heck, give it a try."

"Oh, all right, all right. But remember, this wasn't my idea." Heck glared at the computer as if it were a deadly enemy. Then he began to sing—at least *he* might have called it singing. His effort was completely out of tune with everything.

When he had finished, he frowned at the computer, and the silent computer frowned back. Then he looked around at those watching and said bitterly, "There! You see? That doesn't work either!"

Jerusha did not know exactly how to tell Heck that the problem might be that his singing was so terrible. "I still can't help believing that singing is the answer, though," she said.

Heck looked more pathetic than ever, but then he suddenly brightened. He turned to Dai. "All right, then. *You're* the singer around here, Bando. *You* come and sing to this thing!"

Dai's face registered surprise, but he quickly recovered. "Well . . . OK. I'll do my best. But you'll have to tell me what to say." He came over and stood next to Heck. As the electronics expert fed him the computer instructions, Dai began singing.

Abruptly there was a muted roar. The huge apparatus that filled the center of the room instantly bathed the entire conference area with rays of red light. A steady humming filled the air, a drone so intense that all of the inhabitants grabbed their ears and rubbed them vigorously.

"It's working!" Heck shouted. "It's working! The energy pattern device! It's coming to life!"

Jerusha Ericson was usually a calm individual, but

what she saw next made her feel faint. She gaped as if her eyes had failed her, for what she saw was astounding.

Indeed, they were all speechless and gaping, for the clothes that had been left discarded on the floor or on chairs suddenly began to fill out as if they were being inflated. It was, in a way, like balloons being blown up. Dresses started to swell, men's clothing began to grow plump, suggesting that the air itself inside the conference room was electrified as energy pattern chains were generated by the huge mechanical device.

Mei-Lani seemed convinced that there *was* some sort of electrical current flowing. She touched her hair and found that it rose to meet her fingers.

"Dai," she whispered, "something truly amazing is happening."

Dai grinned triumphantly. He clapped a hand on Heck's shoulder and said, "We've got quite an electronics man here. No one could have done it except you, Heck."

It was an astonishing sight, indeed, and one that neither Space Rangers, nor Petroski, nor any of the youngsters were likely to forget. As the clothes filled out, slowly the outlines of heads and hands began to appear. Then the clothing stood upright, and shoes suddenly aligned themselves beneath trousers and skirts. The planet's inhabitants, who minutes ago had been nothing but a flicker of energy on a piece of plastic, were now being transformed back into flesh and blood human beings.

"I'll never forget this," Raina whispered. "Never."

"None of us will," Mei-Lani agreed.

Jerusha felt like hugging both Dai Bando and Heck. "It's wonderful! It's almost like a new creation."

"It's all scientific enough!" Heck growled. Nevertheless, he was evidently so impressed that tears stood in his eyes. He dashed them away, saying, "Just science. That's all it is."

Jerusha had seen the tears, however, and she put her hand lightly on his arm. "You did fine, Heck Jordan. Real fine. You're a hero."

And then, while there was still time, Dai ran to tell Captain Edge the news.

When the astonished captain arrived, accompanied by Temple Cole and Bronwen, a small but trim man dressed in a pale gray uniform stepped forward to greet him. The man held up his hand in a sign of peace and immediately began to sing.

"He's introducing himself, Captain," Mei-Lani explained quickly. "His name is Captain Tyrone. He's the leader of the colony here."

"My compliments to Captain Tyrone, Mei-Lani. Tell him I can't sing to him. But tell him we're glad to be here."

Mei-Lani sang her interpretation, as Captain Tyrone listened, still apparently wishing to be friendly.

Then the Tyrian captain answered in a clear, high tenor that sounded like a strange, minor key melody.

"He's asking who you are and what has happened."

"I'm afraid one of you who can sing will have to tell him the story."

"Dai's really the best at that," Mei-Lani said.

"But I don't know science well enough to explain stuff," Dai protested. "Heck's the one who really saved the Tyrians and turned them back into people."

There was some confusion, but finally Captain Tyrone, with the assistance of those Rangers who could sing, seemed to understand what had happened. In response, he turned to the group of Space Rangers in particular and sang a lengthy song.

"I wonder what he's saying?" Edge murmured to Temple Cole.

"I don't know, but he's certainly serious about it. Look at his face."

Dai Bando interpreted this time. He looked rather abashed and said, "Captain, I don't know how to say this, but he thinks we're some kind of angels that came to save his people."

Edge grinned. "Well, you'll have to tell him we're not that!"

"I've already told him, and he says if we're not angels then, at least, God sent us."

"Which He did," Raina said. Then she leaned over and said to Bronwen at her side, "Their *singing* sounds angelic, doesn't it?"

"Maybe angels communicate by singing," Dai suggested.

"None of us can know for sure," Bronwen answered. "They *probably* communicate in ways we never dreamed of. Actually, I think all of heaven's going to be like that."

"Like what, Bronwen?"

"It's going to be better than anything we ever thought of or dreamed of. When we see Jesus in His glory, and when we see the heaven He's made for us, it will all be better than we ever could have imagined."

All over the room the happy children, who had by now found their parents, began bringing them to meet the Space Rangers and the officers of the *Daystar*. Dai watched them and, without warning, began to sing—it was the song about the deer panting for the water.

When the song ended, Mei-Lani approached the

Tyrian captain. "Your children know that song," she said. "How does that happen?"

"Many years ago a Christian missionary came through this part of the galaxy," he answered. "We all learned the song. And as we journeyed through space, we sang it again and again and taught it to our children—for, indeed, our hearts pant for the Lord as the deer pants for water."

"I guess it really doesn't matter which planet you're on," Dai mused, "or what color your skin is. Everybody, everywhere in this whole universe, is hungry for God, somehow or other."

"I believe that is true," Mei-Lani agreed. Then she gave Dai an admiring look and said, "And now you see, don't you, that our heavenly Father didn't give you that beautiful voice for nothing. He had a reason."

The compliment obviously embarrassed Dai. He shook his dark head vigorously. "I didn't do much."

"You did what you could. You used what God gave you—and that's all He ever expects of any of us."

14
Endings

The great banquet in the Tyrian conference hall was filled to overflowing. The *Daystar*'s crew was all present, and the officers and the Space Rangers were sitting on a raised platform at the front of the large hall. Even Contessa had been invited and lay quietly by Jerusha's chair.

The hall itself was decorated and looked completely different, due to the efforts of Captain Tyrone, head of the city and the planet itself. It appeared that his people had come out of their electronic state ready and anxious to go to work and totally unharmed by their experiences. They had decorated the hall with colorful streamers of red, yellow, green, and purple, as well as exotic hues that the *Daystar*'s crew had never even imagined.

The entertainment began, and Captain Edge leaned back and listened with satisfaction. "It's beautiful, Temple."

Dr. Cole, sitting next to him, said softly, "I've never heard music like it." She took a sip of juice, one of ten delicious juices that had been provided, and took a deep breath. "I can't believe that there are actually people whose language is song."

"It's like an opera, isn't it? Where everybody sings everything."

"It is—and yet, not exactly like that. Here, *everybody* seems to have a very beautiful, soft, melodious voice. I'd love to learn this tonal language."

"We won't be here long enough for that, I'm afraid."

Temple turned to him. "Why do you say that, Mark? Are we going somewhere soon?"

"Raina picked up a signal from Commandant Winona Lee just before we came to the banquet."

"Can you tell me what it says?"

"Afraid not. The message was locked. And it can't be decoded until we're on our way again, but the commandant sounded pretty edgy. I think it might have something to do with our old friend Richard Irons."

"I can't stand the thought of that man!"

"Neither can I, but I've got a feeling that we're headed for a run-in with him." He speared a piece of white meat and tasted it. "This is delicious. If I could sing, I would ask them what it is."

"Mei-Lani could ask for you. She's already learned so much of the language."

"That girl picks up languages so fast I can't believe it!" He looked down the table at the girl and saw that she was laughing at something Heck Jordan had said. "She's a bright one all right. They all are, all except Dai, of course."

"Dai's smart enough too—in his own way."

"Absolutely. But the rest of the Rangers are more or less geniuses."

"Brilliant they are." Temple looked along the table to where Ringo Smith had his eyes fixed on Raina St. Clair. "But I think Ringo would happily give up his knowledge of computers to be as tall and good-looking as Dai."

"You think so?"

"Don't most of us want something we can't have? We all want to be something we're not. Ringo's no different."

Edge was interested in her remark. He looked down at her. She was wearing an emerald green gown, and jade earrings dangled from the lobes of her ears. Her eyes were clear and beautiful. He said, "I can't imagine you wanting to be anything but what you are."

"That's because you don't know me."

"I thought I was getting to know you pretty well."

Temple Cole said sadly, "It's very hard for one human being to know another one, Mark. I thought I knew someone once, but he—" She broke off. Some unwelcome thought had suddenly come.

"I know someone hurt you along the way, Temple, but you can't live in a cave and cut yourself off from life because of that."

Forcing a smile, she said, "All right. Now let's talk about something else besides me."

The entertainment that the Tyrian captain provided had been mostly singing, but there were also dances—graceful dances—and some of the children joined in.

Watching the boys and girls perform, Dai said to Raina, who sat to his right, "They're very skilled."

"Yes, they are." Then Raina looked at him and said brightly, "Ballet dancing is something *you'd* be good at, Dai."

"Why would you ever think that?"

"Because you're good at anything that requires agility."

"Well, I never cared much for ballet." He looked around the hall, and Raina saw satisfaction leap into his eyes. "I feel good about what we did. We accomplished something important on this voyage."

"Yes, we did, Dai," Raina said. "I really believe that God sent us here."

141

"I think He did, too. And I hope the next voyage will be as good as this one."

At that moment Captain Edge was introduced by the Tyrian leader.

Edge stood behind his chair and said, "I'm sorry that I don't speak your beautiful language." He waited for Mei-Lani to interpret, then went on to make a brief speech. He spoke of the future of Ciephus. And he concluded by saying, "I must tell you how proud I am of my crew, especially of Ensign Heck Jordan. He was the one who discovered the red comet, and it was he who was able to get the information about your people from the computers."

Heck looked at Raina with pride, but she shook her head negatively at him.

When the speeches were over, Mei-Lani whispered to Raina, "What Heck did *was* important, but if it hadn't been for Dai's singing, the city wouldn't have been saved. It was really Dai's singing, wasn't it?"

"I think it was really the Lord," Raina replied, "who saved the day for the crimson people. Not any of us. We were just His instruments."

After dinner, the *Daystar* people moved around among the inhabitants of the planet, though most could speak very little of the language, especially those who had no talent for singing, such as Heck.

Edge and Temple stayed close to Mei-Lani, who served as their translator. He saw Jerusha across the room. She also had picked up some of the language, and she was interpreting for others.

Later, the captain saw Jerusha lurking back in a corner, and he thought, *She looks lonely. I wonder what's wrong with her.* Temple Cole was engaged in conversation with one of the older members of the colony, and he left her side to go over to where Jerusha stood. Warily, he looked down at Contessa, whose tail began thumping against the floor.

"Don't you let that animal get at me, Jerusha."

"Be still, Contessa." The dog's tail continued to thump, and she stood up, but she made no attempt to put her paws on Edge's chest—which she loved to do.

Edge glared at the big German shepherd. "I can't understand it. I've done everything I can to discourage this female, and still she won't let me alone."

"You have charms, Captain Edge, for females."

Jerusha's words were spoken with some sort of irony that he couldn't quite interpret. Edge said, "Is that some sort of wisecrack, Lieutenant Ericson?"

"Not at all. You can see how much she likes you. I don't imagine you ever find it hard to get females to like you."

"What kind of rumors have you been listening to?" he asked suspiciously.

Jerusha smiled slightly. "None at all, Captain. I don't listen to rumors."

"Well, it sounded like some sort of wisecrack. And what are you doing over here in the corner all by yourself, anyway? Come on out and join the party."

"I—I don't really care to do that. I've had enough party."

Edge was puzzled. He knew that Jerusha was a very outgoing girl. He knew she was also sensitive to the moods of people—especially his. So he asked, "You're not picking up some bad vibes from me, are you?"

"I do think you're troubled about something, Captain, but I don't expect you to tell me about it."

"Jerusha, it's just that—" Edge stopped, then shrugged. "Nothing's secret about it, really. It's just that we'll be leaving here shortly. We've just received a sealed message from Commandant Lee. I won't know where we're going, or why, until we're under way."

"I could tell that something was troubling you. Every time you're worried, you rub your right wrist."

Edge, who was doing exactly that, whipped his hand down and scowled at her. "I'll have to remember not to do that again!"

"You do other things too."

"Like what?"

"Oh, I don't think I'll tell you. I like to be able to know what you're up to."

Edge gave her a crooked smile and then let his gaze wander back over the banquet room. He enjoyed the sight of his crew mingling with the inhabitants of the colony. "When I first came to get you, Jerusha, in that run-down room you were living in, I bet you never thought we'd be here on the planet Ciephus having a party with a bunch of red people. Did you?"

"No, I certainly didn't."

"Are you glad you joined the *Daystar* crew?"

"Y–yes." Jerusha's answer was quiet, and she faltered slightly.

"You don't sound very sure about it!"

"Well, I'm not at my best right now, Captain."

Captain Mark Edge was a good captain, but he did not know much about girls. If he had, he would have realized that fifteen-year-old Jerusha Ericson had developed a crush on him. He simply thought of her as a girl who was on the verge of womanhood and who would someday be very attractive. He felt like an old man as he stood beside her, but he could not know that this troubled her greatly.

"Well," he said, "I'm going back and join the party. I wish you'd come with me."

"Maybe I will," she said. "Can Contessa come, too?"

"As long as she doesn't shove me into any table!"

Jerusha suddenly laughed. "I remember when she did that at our first party. You looked so funny with food all over your uniform."

"I can laugh about it now," he said. "Just don't let her do it again."

Captain Edge and Jerusha rejoined the party. Shortly thereafter the festivities were over, and after a series of formal and informal good-byes, the crew returned to the *Daystar*.

Bronwen looked across at Dai, sitting opposite her. Her nephew often came to her cabin to talk about the Bible and listen to her tell stories of the old days back on Earth—and about their family.

Dai had sung several songs for her, but then he fell silent. "I don't know what God's going to do with my life, Aunt," he said presently. "I don't seem to fit into being a *Daystar* Space Ranger. I can't run computers, for example. That side of my brain seems to be dead."

"Maybe it is," Bronwen said gently. She walked around to him and caressed his dark hair. "You look very much like your father, Dai," she whispered. "I loved him very much. He was the best brother I ever knew."

"I miss him, too, though I can't remember much about him."

"And you're really worried about what God wants to do with your life?"

"I am. I wish He would speak to me directly—tell me what He wants me to do. I know He doesn't often do that anymore, but . . ."

"No, God rarely gives guidance that way. But you

remember what Proverbs three, five and six, says: 'Trust in the Lord with all your heart and do not lean on your own understanding. In all your ways acknowledge Him, and He will make your paths straight.'"

Dai grinned. "Sure, I remember. I've got that one memorized. You've drilled it into me enough."

"Come along, Dai. Let's go have a look at God's heavens."

They walked together down the corridor to the *Daystar*'s observatory. Outside, the stars were spread out like glittering diamonds, and the two stood in silence, marveling at the countless points of light. Toward the southeast, the massive green wings of the Great Orion Nebula spread into the heavens as far as the eye could see. The brightest star in the winter sky, Sirius, could be seen just to the right of the nebula's dovelike head.

"I guess it boils down to this," Dai said. "If God can make all of this, He can take care of one insignificant ensign."

Bronwen gave him a sudden hug. "You're not so little. Not in His sight, Dai Bando."

"Captain Edge says we have a new assignment. I don't know where we're going," he said with sudden confidence, "but wherever it is, I know God will be with us."

"Amen to that."

Neither spoke for a while. They simply stood in the quiet darkness, looking out at the stars.

Then Bronwen said, "I have a feeling that we're headed into some sort of danger, worse than anything we've known, Dai."

"What kind of danger?"

"I don't know about that, but I think all of the *Daystar* Space Rangers—indeed, the whole crew—

had better be prepared for something . . . terrifying."

Dai laid his hand lightly on her shoulder and said, "I'm glad you're here, Aunt."

"I'm glad you're here, too, Dai. Whatever is coming, we'll go through it together."

The two continued to watch the sky. Soon they would be out in space again. Otherwise, the future was hidden from them. But whatever happened, they would need—and have—the hand of God to keep them safe.

Moody Press, a ministry of the Moody Bible Institute,
is designed for education, evangelization, and edification.
If we may assist you in knowing more about Christ
and the Christian life, please write us without obligation:
Moody Press, c/o MLM, Chicago, Illinois 60610.